Alice Where Art Thou?

Elizabeth Cadell

The Friendly Air Publishing

thefriendlyairpublishing.com

This book is a work of fiction. Names, locals, business, organizations, and incidents are products of the author's imagination or are used fictitiously. Any resemblance to actual events, locals, or persons, living or dead, is entirely coincidental.

Cover art by Aparna Bera

Chapter One

I'd had just a week in which to find a flat nice enough, comfortable enough and central enough for Chess and myself to live in. This was the sixth day of the search; I had concentrated on the less expensive districts of London and I had seen twenty-three flats and I was feeling almost dead with exhaustion—but I had to go on until I found one. Chess was depending on me.

Of the places I'd looked at, the majority had been terrible, but a few would have suited us; the search would have been over if there hadn't been one other all-important requisite: the place had to be cheap.

Six days; twenty-three flats. And now I stood facing the landlady of the twenty-fourth flat and I knew that at last I'd found something that would meet all our requirements except one: price. The rent was higher than the one Chess and I had fixed on as our absolute maximum—but I argued persuasively to myself that it wasn't far off it.

The flat was the top floor of a house that had been converted into three almost self-contained apartments. The rooms were large, with high ceilings, and would probably be piercingly cold in winter—but this was May; we needn't worry about winter yet.

The accommodation was on both sides of the staircase; the drawing room was on one side, the remaining rooms on the other, which meant that we should have to cross the landing every time we wanted to go from the drawing room to the kitchen or the bedrooms. On a lower floor, this would have involved the risk of meeting—perhaps in a state of undress—anybody who happened to be going up or downstairs, but this was the top flat and no such inconvenience attached to it; we could move to and fro freely, for the only people who would use the last flight of stairs would be our own visitors.

I liked the drawing room. It had four large windows, two of which, unfortunately, overlooked Stacey Street, which was a neighbourhood so shabby as to merit the name slum; but the two windows on the other side, coming down almost to floor level, looked out on to trim, pleasant Stacey Square. Outside both sets of windows was a balcony on which I visualised spending warm summer evenings.

Across the landing, the other rooms lacked the spaciousness of the drawing room, but I liked the way in which the two original rooms had been converted. There was a bedroom with two beds in it; another room so small that it fitted nothing more than a bed and a cupboard; a bathroom and a lavatory. None of it was smart or modern; the furniture was terrible and the curtains looked like dyed sheets, but the flat had something I hadn't been offered anywhere else: airiness and cleanliness.

It was so clean that it shone.

It would, I was certain, suit us very well—but the rent was higher than we could or should pay. I looked at the landlady and braced myself to try a little bargaining.

It didn't look too hopeful. She was called Mrs. Flower, which was misleading, for she was quite colourless: mousey hair, sallow skin and rather washed-out grey eyes. She was dressed in a black coat and skirt with a white nylon blouse. She was younger than the other landladies I'd seen; she couldn't, I thought, have been much over thirty.

She hadn't said a word since she let me in. We had gone up the stairs in complete silence, and in silence she had opened one door after another and led me through the rooms. She'd watched me wordlessly as I'd pretended to be the kind of young woman nobody can do down: I'd pressed the springs of the beds, and I'd begun to examine the kitchen fittings, but she raised an eyebrow and pulled her lips into a straight, sardonic line and I gave up. When we'd been round the flat twice, we stood in the drawing room and she waited for me to speak.

"I like the flat," I said frankly, "but it's more than I can afford."

"Pity," remarked Mrs. Flower dryly. Her accent was that of the North and she had a faintly smug look, as though nobody had ever succeeded in getting the better of her.

"Is there any chance—"

"None whatsoever," she said. "You knew the rent before

ever you got here, and I told the agents I wasn't going to reduce it. Payable monthly in advance."

"I like it," I said again, " but there are only going to be two of us in it and—"

"Who's the two?" she broke in to ask.

"Myself and another girl."

She gave a sound I can only call a snort, and marched to the door and opened it.

"You should've said so in the first place," she said. "No girls. No girls on their own, I distinctly said to the agents. No business girls messing up my flats, that's what I told them. I tried it once, but never again. They did all but wreck the place. I thought you were the girl who was coming to look the place over for her parents—aren't you Miss Walker?"

"No."

"Then we've both been wasting our time," said Mrs. Flower. "I don't know what you do with yours, but mine's valuable. I run a coffee bar in the King's Road and I'm sick and tired of being called out of it to show people round for nothing. I know you girls; you come from homes where your mother's been doing everything for you, and you take a flat and a job to pass the time, and you entertain your boyfriends and never give a moment to keeping a decent place in order. I'd rather let a troop of Siamese cats through here than a couple of you girls."

"I see," I said, in what I hoped was a quiet and dignified tone.

We walked in silence down the stairs. She opened the front door and gave me a look half angry, half apologetic.

"You get sick to death of showing people round," she said.

"You get sick to death of being shown round," I told her. "This was the first flat I've seen that I wouldn't have minded living in."

I don't know whether she would have replied, or merely shown me out—but at that moment a taxi stopped outside and a girl stepped out of it. In a loud, ludicrously affected voice, she directed the driver to wait, and then came up the four steps of the entrance and stood before us.

Mrs. Flower and I looked at her. She was slender and smart and on her face was the entire cosmetics calendar: powder base, powder, rouge, eye-shadow, mascara, eyebrow pencil, lipstick ... as I said, everything. She was haughty and commanding. She must have been quite eighteen. She gave us both a look of disdain and said:

"I am Miss Walkah. I have an ordah to view."

I was so enraptured that I had forgotten where I was, but Mrs. Flower brought me back with a jolt.

"You're too late," she told the new arrival, in her most abrupt manner. "The flat's let. Good morning."

She shut the door with a bang. Miss Walker was outside—and I was in.

"Come upstairs," said Mrs. Flower.

In the drawing room, she stood and looked me over.

"There are girls and girls," she said. "If you were like that one . . . but you're not."

"Wasn't she just looking the place over for her parents?"

"If they turned that out as a daughter ..."

I could have told her that parents didn't really have much say in how their daughters turned out. Instead, I said:

"I think I'm a domestic type. I've shared a flat with girls before and I kept it in good order. I like this place because I think it'll be easy to keep clean; there's not much furniture, and—"

"—and no knick-knacks. They're a curse."

"—and the kitchen's convenient and it's got a nice new sink—"

"—which I hope you won't go and chip. It chips if you bang a heavy saucepan down on it. You can't have big parties here."

"I don't think I can promise to—"

"I didn't mean parties; I meant dances. Those girls who were here invited their men friends and they turned back the carpet and danced. Like Bedlam, it was. I came up and put a stop to it."

"Do you live here?" I asked.

"Yes. We live in the ground floor flat, Mr. Flower and me. I'm out all day at the coffee bar; Mr. Flower works there mornings and evenings, but in the daytime he cleans up here and fixes up anything that wants fixing in the flats. If anything goes wrong, don't try messing about with it; tell Mr. Flower and he'll see to it."

"Who lives on the middle floor?" I asked.

"South American couple. They've just opened a Spanish leather shop up at the top of Sloane Street. They're very quiet; they're both out all day. I hope you'll be as—"

She stopped abruptly. I had drawn off a glove, and she had seen my ring.

"But you're engaged," she said.

"Yes. So is the girl who's going to live with me."

"You should've said so before," said Mrs. Flower in a tone of relief. "That makes all the difference. Two engaged girls . . . that means there won't be that string of men coming and going. You'll—" Her eyes narrowed. "But if you're engaged, what're you taking a flat for? Not less than a year's lease; I made that plain to the agents."

"We're not getting married for a year or so; we're hoping to get jobs in London in the meantime."

"I see. Where's your young man?"

"In Malaya."

"And the other one?"

"In New York."

"I see," said Mrs. Flower again. " Well, subject to everything being all right, you can come. You're taking it for a year?"

I said that I was, and she led me downstairs to her flat.

While she got a pencil and paper and prepared to take down some particulars, I looked round and saw that her living room was as bare as the rooms upstairs had been. Mrs. Flower's dislike of knick-knacks would account for the absence of a single ornament, but there was not a book, not a vase, not a picture—not a sign of habitation. It was about as homelike as a cell.

She must have seen my glance.

"The way to keep tidy," she said, "is to put things away in cupboards. It takes no time at all to clean up here when we've had our breakfast. 'Tisn't as if we were at home much."

I wondered what Mr. Flower was like, and whether he liked living in a bare and cheerless flat with a hard-faced wife who kept everything in cupboards. But Mrs. Flower was asking more questions.

"Name and address? "

"My name's O'Connell."

"Christian name?"

"My initials are D. C."

Miss D. C. O'Connell, she wrote, and I waited. She made no sign, but sometimes there was a double-take; sometimes even the initials brought on the slow, puzzled frown and the almost inevitable question: " O'Connell . . . Denise, would it be? Then you must be the daughter of . . ."

And after that, a rush of eager, breathless questions and an outpouring of adulation and a closing-in of those nearby to hear and to see better. . . But Mrs. Flower, managing her house and her coffee bar and, it seemed, her husband, obviously hadn't time to read theatrical gossip. For the first time, I felt a very small stir of liking for her.

As soon as I got away, I rang up Chess. Her name is Francesca, pronounced the Italian way—but her parents were the only ones who have ever pronounced it. To everybody else she has been, all her life, simply Chess.

"I've got one," I told her.

"Oh, Denny!" The name was long drawn out; Chess's voice was almost hoarse with relief. "You mean it's definite?"

"I'm signing the lease tomorrow. You said a year, and that's how long it's going to be, but—"

"Yes, I know; you said all that before. What's a year?"

"Have it your own way," I said. "But when Stephen gets back from New York—"

"What's the flat like?"

"It's not smart. It's—"

"Who cares about smart? What's the rent? "

I told her, and there was a long pause. Then:

"But . . . but just between the two of us—"

"It was the cheapest one I saw. I mean, it was the cheapest that would do. And it was by far the nicest. But if you feel it'll be too much—"

"I feel it's too much and you feel it's too long; that makes us even," said Chess. "We'll take it; if we can't pay, all they can do is turn us out—I hope. What else?"

"It's a top flat. It's got shabby furniture and cheap curtains, but it's full of light and air."

"That's what we'll be full of when we've paid the rent. Where is it?"

"18 Stacey Square, Chelsea, S.W. 3."

"Where's Stacey Square?"

"Practically off the King's Road. You know that arty-crafty shop with the loom in the window? Well, you turn down the street it's on the corner of, and you—"

"Chamier Street?"

"Yes. It's at the top of that. One side of the Square is terribly dingy, but the other side's nice, and the house itself is quite decent."

"Who else lives there?"

"A South American couple in the middle, and the landlady and her husband on the ground. There's no basement. We only got the place because we're both engaged, which means we won't—she says—entertain men, which means—she says—no heavy treads at night."

"Are there sheets and things?"

"Everything—of a kind. Tin spoons and forks."

"Denny, when can we move in?"

"As soon as the lease is signed."

"I know we can't afford it, but—"

"At the moment we can't. But we've got to live somewhere, and once we've both got jobs and there's some money coming in—"

"If I come up the day after tomorrow, can we move in?"

"I don't see why we shouldn't. Mrs. Flower's doing the inventory, to save the fee; the place is practically bare, so it shouldn't take long."

"I'll meet you on Wednesday, some time during the morning—at our flat," said Chess. "Our flat . . . Oh, Denny, isn't it going to be heaven?"

I began to say that I didn't think so, as Heaven was a place where people weren't likely to be worried about food and rent bills, but she had rung off.

By Tuesday, I'd signed the lease, gone over the inventory and got the keys. The checking of the inventory was done not by Mrs. Flower, but by her husband, a small, thin little man who could have walked on just as he was in one of my mother's productions and taken the part of the spiritless husband cowed by a managing wife. He was about forty; he had stooping shoulders, an apologetic manner and watery light-blue eyes. He spoke with a Cockney accent and called me Miss, but before we were through with the inventory, we both knew that we liked one another.

He signed, and I signed, and then he led me downstairs.

" 'Ope you'll be comfy, you and your friend, Miss," he said as we went. "Place is bare, o' course, but I dare say you'll soon have your little things all spread out, looking ever-so homey. Going to get married, the two of you, the wife tells me."

"Not just yet," I said.

"Well, one of 'em's a lucky man," stated Mr. Flower, as he opened the front door. "You look to me, if I may say so, Miss, a nice sensible young lady."

I thanked him and said that I would take possession on the following day, and he promised to be there.

"To see you in," he explained.

But it was Mrs. Flower who saw me in. Giving me possession, she had several orders to issue: her bedroom being on one side of the front door, she was not to be disturbed at night by farewells on the front doorstep, car engines, car doors, loud laughter or chatty exchanges. Upstairs, we were not to tread heavily or to bang doors. We were to put the garbage bucket out in the back yard before ten o'clock each morning and remove our milk bottles from the hall before nine. Never were we to go on to the balcony outside the drawing room windows, for it had lost its underpinning and was extremely dangerous; she had repeatedly asked the builders to come and repair it and they would do so in time—their own time.

I listened to all this, and nodded. Mrs. Flower hung about for a time in the hope, I think, of seeing Chess arrive, but Chess was late and eventually she went back to her coffee bar.

And then the doorbell gave a loud and prolonged buzz and I went downstairs at a run and let Chess in and stood for a moment in the hall giving myself the pleasure of looking at her.

We had not met for two years, but I found her unchanged. Tall and far too thin, she looked like one of those sketches in the couturier section of *Vogue;* only a line or two, but an impression of cool, poised elegance. Chess was neither cool nor poised nor elegant, but that was the way she struck people at first sight.

We were school friends—but not childhood friends. The school at which we had met five years ago, when we were both nineteen, was Madame Narvik's School for Young Ladies in Florence. It was not a finishing school; as Madame Narvik explained to the young ladies on the first day of term, she could not finish something that had not begun.

What had not begun was our education. There were thirty of us, all carefully selected; we were all the daughters of parents who, for one reason or another, had been too preoccupied with more important matters to notice until we were almost out of our teens that— apart from a smattering of geography picked up when some of us had wandered with our parents from place to place—our minds were a total blank. Madame Narvik, with this unpromising material, undertook to do no more than fill, as well as she could, the gaps in our appreciation of the arts. By the arts she meant painting and architecture.

So we arrived at the amber-coloured, dilapidated old Palace with balconies that looked over the Arno and from which, glancing to the left, we could see the Ponte Vecchio. When we had unpacked and settled down, three or four in a bedroom, Madame Narvik turned us loose in the Uffizi Gallery, without guidebook or guide, and told us to return in three hours and write down which picture we had liked best, and why. We went on from there. She took us in batches to Rome, to Venice, to Ravenna, to Paris and Madrid. We gazed and we gazed, and then we began to read, and at this sign of awakening intellect, Madame Narvik summoned her professors and we began to learn.

Apart from the pictures and the buildings, our life was our own. She hadn't, said Madame, undertaken to teach us manners or morals. If any girl behaved in a way which Madame termed indelicate—the word covered everything from personal hygiene to perverted habits—the offender was out, so swiftly that one moment she was there and the next, her place had been taken by somebody from the waiting list, which was as long as the Amazon.

There were three girls in my room: myself, Chess and a girl called Marya Annuzio. Chess was the only titled girl in the school; Madame said that she disliked titles as they gave the school an undesirable snob value—but Chess said the real reason she disliked them was because no aristocrat nowadays could afford to pay the astronomical fees. Chess's were paid by a plebeian aunt. Her parents had left England twenty years earlier to look for a place that was cheap, that had a mild, sunny climate all the year round, that was in the sterling area, that had no dangerous animals or unpleasant insects and in which there was a colony of quiet, well-bred English people, an English Church and safe drinking water. They were still looking.

Marya Annuzio was an Argentinian. Her father was a self-made millionaire with business interests in several European capitals, and Marya had seen little of her South American home. Her mother, like my father, seemed to have melted away after a year or so of marriage.

When we had been three years with Madame Narvik, the three of us separated—reluctantly; we had become, without realising it, a closely-knit trio. We were all three different in race and in temperament, but somehow, we fitted. When we left Florence, we tried to keep in touch with one another, but I was the only one who wrote regularly. Marya's letters were almost always written on trains or in planes, promising more when she got to wherever it was she was going. Chess was one of those people who assemble paper, envelopes and stamps and then sit for hours waiting for inspiration that never comes.

And here was Chess, and here I was, and we were both glad.

She went up the stairs and I followed, looking at her long, straight back and long, lovely legs. Everything about her was long: hands, feet, face. I've seen earl's daughters who look totally unlike the popular conception of how they ought to look—but when you looked at Chess, you had a feeling, whether you cared for her looks or not, that she was the end product of some exceedingly elegant unions.

"This," I said, opening the door, "is the drawing room."

But Chess wasn't ready to look at it. She flung herself on to the sofa in a way that would have enraged Mrs. Flower, and gazed up at me.

"If you knew what it meant to be here ..." she said slowly.

"I do know," I said. " I only wish I'd done it sooner."

"Then why didn't you?"

"Lots of reasons. Money, first of all. When I had a job in London two years ago, I found I couldn't live on my novice's salary. I had to wait; I had to get a bit more experience. That's why, when one of the directors offered me a job in the Rome office, I took it. I knew he needed me more outside the office than in it; I spoke Italian and I did all the running round for himself and his wife. When I got engaged, I gave in my notice and got a good reference—and here I am."

"Your letter," said Chess, in the same slow voice, "was like a . . . like a lifeline."

I sat on the arm of a chair and looked at her.

"As bad as that? " I asked.

"Yes. I don't want to harrow you," said Chess, " but I've often felt, lately, that those wonderful years at Narvik's were being cancelled out by my having to live with my aunt and repay her for having paid my fees."

She closed her eyes and I saw her fingers moving as she counted. "Twenty-three months of it, Denny," she said, opening her eyes and fixing them on me. "Think of it. In Bath, of all places, living like the ghost of a Jane Austen heroine. I thought she'd paid my fees out of kindness, but all she was doing was investing the money to get herself an unpaid companion later on."

"Couldn't you have joined your parents?"

"I even, if you'll believe it, went so far as to write to them and suggest it. They were in Bermuda. They wrote back to say that I owed my aunt a great deal and I ought to be glad to pay it back. One day, they said, they might be able to send for me—but at present they were in an hotel, and cottages were expensive and hard to come by, but as soon as they got the offer of a cheap one . . . and so on and so on."

"But—"

"Then at last I got desperate and told my aunt that I'd like to leave her. I knew you were coming home— I mean coming back to England, and when you said you were going to take a flat and wanted me to share it . . ."

"You told your aunt you wanted to leave—" I prompted.

"Yes. That was between knowing you were coming home, and getting your letter. I told her I was going—and her answer was to tell me that she was going to shut up the house in a week and go abroad. She thought I'd have nowhere to go."

"That's why I had to get this flat in such a hurry?"

"Yes." She rose. "Go on showing me."

"Well, take a look at the drawing room," I said. "It's a drawing and dining room, both; we open up that folding table and eat off it—if we can afford to eat."

She looked round the room. There was nothing to be learned from her expression, because she doesn't at any time register any. Some people think that she always looks blank to the point of idiocy, but to me, part of the fun of knowing her is waiting to find out what she's thinking—if she's thinking.

"Nice," she said at last. "Light and airy, just as you said. Nice for entertaining. We can hire another chair or two and—"

"No entertaining," I said. "Come across the landing; the other rooms are on the other side."

"What I like," she said, seating herself on the edge of the kitchen table at the end of our tour, "is the way you can shut off this side of the flat. I mean, if I'm entertaining someone who bores you, you can go to bed, and when I come into the kitchen to get drinks or sandwiches or anything, you'll be beyond the closed door, with the bedrooms and the bath and the lav, all nice and self-contained. Why does the phone have to be in the corridor outside the bathroom?"

"That's one of the nice things; there are two phones. One in this part and the other in the drawing room."

"You mean an extension?"

"Yes."

"Nicely thought out," she said approvingly. "Which of us is having the bedroom and which of us is sleeping in the sarcophagus?"

"I thought it might be sensible to share the bedroom," I said. "We could push the beds to the wall instead of having them together like that, and then we could use the tiny room as a sort of dressing room."

Chess walked into it and looked round.

"Pity we couldn't have put Marya in it," she said.

"Not exactly her standard, is it?" I asked. "Do you ever hear from her?"

"Now and then. Funny she's not married, isn't it? Must be what they call an embarrassment of choice. How about writing to her and suggesting—"

"—her coming here? Can you honestly imagine Marya in this flat?"

"Honestly I can't imagine," said Chess gloomily. "But it would have been nice to use some of her money."

But as we couldn't, we went on by ourselves for four weeks, and it was as cosy as could be—and then the bill for the next month's rent came in, and we couldn't pay it.

By that time, we'd both got jobs. Chess was working in Mrs. Flower's coffee bar, and I was secretary to a managing director in the City. I got a good salary and Chess made a lot in tips, and when the end of the week came, we felt rich. But by Wednesday of each week, we were out of money. We budgeted, we watched every penny, we scrimped—but always by Wednesday we had spent our last shilling.

We looked at the rent bill and Chess turned pale.

"How?" she asked me.

I couldn't tell her.

It might be supposed that two girls, one a peer's daughter, the other the only child of Denise O'Connell, England's most loved, most successful actress, could between them produce thirty-two pounds to pay a month's rent for a furnished flat. But the Earl was all but insolvent, and all the money Chess could rely on was an occasional sum wrung out of him, and the crumbs that fell from her aunt's cheque book. Since she had left her aunt, these crumbs no longer fell. For myself, things were even worse; the allowance I got from my father had been fixed eighteen years ago and had never been brought into line with present-day prices.

I could have got more money. My stepfathers, who succeeded one another with monotonous regularity, would have been glad to keep me in comfort, not to say luxury; but I had an obstinate and probably stupid idea that I preferred to live on my father's money. I liked my stepfathers, but from the moment I became old enough to size up the general situation, I had made up my mind that as soon as I was out of school, I would live on what my father had agreed to give me, plus whatever I could earn.

Nobody seemed to know what had become of my original father. When I was very young, I gleaned from whispered comments here and there that he had skipped off about a year after his marriage to my mother, leaving her with the baby, but without means to support the poor little thing. Later, I learned that he had arranged a yearly allowance for me. Later still, my mother's brother, Uncle Philip, whom I love dearly and who has been as good as a father to me all my life, dropped casually, from time to time, news items about my father: he was in Egypt, he was in Singapore, he was here and there in the various branches of his commercial pursuits—but he was never, I gathered, in England. He seemed—apart from the allowance—to have no interest in me, and it was only lately that I had found myself with a slowly growing desire to learn something about him and the circumstances of the brief marriage. The more I knew of my mother, the more I wanted to know about my father.

But in the meantime there was the money situation, and it was serious.

"You could get the money out of your Uncle Philip," Chess said after a time. "He'll be back in England soon."

"No."

"Why not?"

"Because I know perfectly well that he's in touch with my father. If I ask him for money, he'll ask my father to raise my allowance."

"And what, for heaven's sake, is wrong with that? "

"If my father offers it, I'll take more—but I won't ask for it."

"That attitude," said Chess in a tone of exasperation, "is one of what they call sinful pride. It's the only happy solution, and you won't accept it."

"No, I won't. But there must be other ways. Couldn't we

write to your parents and—"

"No."

There was complete finality in her tone, and I didn't press the point.

"So what do we do? " I asked.

"I suppose we could look for a cheaper flat."

"You've forgotten—we signed a lease. We're stuck with this one for a year."

"Good," said Chess with deep satisfaction. " I like it here."

"Yes, but—"

There was no point in going on. Chess had drifted into the bathroom and had turned on the taps for her bath. For some time the water ran, making speech impossible.

"I tell you what," she called when the noise had stopped. "I've got an idea. We could—"

I never learned what we could have done. The door buzzer had given the sudden rude noise that always made me jump three feet into the air.

I looked at my watch: ten-thirty p.m.

"Who on earth—?" I called to Chess.

"It might be my cousin Lance; he sometimes comes up to town. Let him in," directed Chess.

"At this time of night?"

"Yes—hurry. Don't let him get away. He's over forty, and terribly boring, but he knows a lot of men. Perhaps he'll produce some for us."

"But—"

"Oh, Denny, hurry! Don't argue! You want to *see* people, don't you? We've been here a whole month and we haven't set eyes on a man. Go on down and bring him up. I'll be out in a minute. Hurry!"

I hurried. There had been two or three more prolonged buzzes—so persistent, that as I went downstairs, I framed several sentences designed to fry Chess's cousin where he stood.

I opened the front door.

On the doorstep was not a man, but a girl; a girl so lovely that even through my astonishment I found myself with the same feeling of detached pleasure I'd had when I first met her over five years ago.

"M-Marya!" I stammered. "What on earth—"

"Hello, Denny."

Her greeting was as casual as though she'd been invited to drop in for a drink. I could only stare at her, and I heard her laugh.

"You haven't changed," she said. "You look just the same."

I'd forgotten her voice—loud, almost strident, and with a strong foreign accent.

"What are you doing here?" I asked.

"First let me in," she said, "and then ask these questions." She jerked her chin towards the taxi that waited outside. "Pay for that, Denny."

I half turned to go up and get some money, but she stopped

me.

"Not now. When the man has taken up the luggage."

Taking my eyes, with an effort, off Marya, I counted the pieces and grew pale.

"We'll have to leave it in the hall for tonight," I said. " Mr. Flower—the landlord—can help us up with it in the morning."

But the taxi driver, who would, I knew, have refused to carry up so much as my handbag, was already halfway up the stairs with two of Marya's matching cases. Chess, hearing the stir, hearing Marya's voice, came out of the bathroom in a rush, one of Mrs. Flower's inadequate bath towels clutched round her. The driver stared at her and, panting more than ever, went down for more luggage, colliding at the bend of the staircase with an enraged Mrs. Flower, on her way up to see what all the noise was about. Behind her, sensibly carrying up more luggage, came little Mr. Flower. Below him appeared the dressing-gowned figure of the South American who lived on the floor below; after a few protesting words, he caught sight of Marya, stopped dead in the middle of a sentence and then bounded up the stairs, giving out a rippling cascade of Spanish through which the name Marya sounded like a peal of welcome. After him came his wife; Marya was embraced by them both, and then embraced again, to the accompaniment of their three voices raised in loud, overjoyed exchange.

In the end, it was Mrs. Flower who had to pay the taxi driver. When all the commotion had subsided, when the hall and landings had been cleared, when Mr. and Mrs. Flower and the taxi driver and the South American couple had gone away, Chess and I stood in the drawing room and looked at Marya and she looked at us.

Nature, which sketched Chess lightly, did a more thorough job on Marya. Here was no long, faint line, no impression of length and leanness. Marya was built much closer to the ground, and built beautifully. If Chess was a long, flowing river, Marya was a short, curving one offering glimpses of lovely light and shadow, teasing the mind with visions of warm, sunlit patches and cool, withdrawn, hidden banks. Her figure was enough in itself to draw all eyes—but it was her colouring that I had always found the most alluring part of her: black, black hair, the creamiest of skins, eyes of black velvet, heavily fringed, and a mouth, soft and full and red, that would have sent me dizzy if I had been a man.

Her gaze went round the drawing room. Chess and I had done, we thought, wonders with it; we'd bought cheap but passable pictures from little dim shops in the King's Road; we'd burrowed through second-hand china shops in Kensington and found pseudo-Chinese vases, and arranged them with their chips and cracks hidden. We'd even bought a two-foot-high china figure of a Japanese lady with a kimono and fan, and we'd picked up two crystal balls which made very fine bookends. We thought the place was transformed—but it was clear that Marya was not impressed; her gaze was on the drab curtains, the shabby, patched chair covers, the worn carpet and threadbare hearthrug. Her face, unlike Chess's, is very expressive.

"This apartment is not *chic*," she said at last.

"We know that," said Chess, "but we couldn't afford anything *chic*-er. In fact, we can't afford this one."

"There's no proper bedroom for you," I told Marya. "If you're staying the night—"

"The night?" broke in Marya. "But I am staying here always."

There was a long pause.

"Say that again," said Chess at last.

Marya looked from one to the other.

"I have come to stay here with you," she said. " You want me, no?"

"We want you, yes," said Chess. " But you'll have to pay."

"Pay ?" Marya raised her shoulders in a slow shrug, raised her eyebrows and brought up her hands, palms upward. I never saw a gesture that said so much.

"You don't mean," said Chess, aghast, "that—"

"You wrote to me and you said that you had an apartment," explained Marya, "and I decided at once that I shall come. If you had done this long ago, I should have come then; I have been wishing that you would do this."

"You mean you've . . . you've come to share the flat with us?" I asked.

"Share the flat? Yes. I did not know that you would ask me to share some money too," answered Marya. "You mean that you wish me to give you money? "

"That's what we wish," said Chess. "What's the hitch? "

"Please?"

"The hitch. The . . . Do you mean you don't want to pay? "

"Want? Of course I want," said Marya. "But I cannot. I have quarrelled with my father. When I said that I wished to come and live here with you, he became very angry. He refused to give me money. So I borrowed from my friends. It was not enough for me to fly and so I came on a ship. I spent the money for my fare, and now I have nothing."

"But—" Chess looked at the piles of luggage and spoke hopefully. " What's in all those cases ? Clothes worth thousands, I bet."

"Clothes?" Marya shrugged indifferently. "Clothes I have, yes; money, no."

So that made three of us in Mrs. Flower's house, and as we cleared what space we could in the cupboards to make room for Marya's things; as we sat on her narrow bed in the tiny room watching her getting ready for bed; as we followed her into the bathroom and out again, talking, talking, talking all the time, we all felt happy and carefree. We were together once more, and it was fun. We were together, and things would work out somehow and there was no need to worry—yet. We were together, and everything would be all right. Our only trouble would be lack of money.

But that wasn't going to be the worst trouble.

Chapter Two

With the coming of Marya, the pace of life at the flat changed abruptly.

During the first month of our tenancy, Chess and I had lived very quietly. We had spent our first week unpacking and settling in; the second week had gone in looking for jobs and the third and fourth weeks in shaking down into a routine. Nobody had visited us; my mother was at her villa in Cap Ferrat; my Uncle Philip was abroad on business; Chess's parents were still in Bermuda. We had friends we could have rung up, but they were not close friends and they were not, Chess pointed out, men friends; we would be much better off without them.

Then Marya joined us, and at once the phone began to ring and kept on ringing; people arrived and kept on arriving. Men, young and not so young, rang the front door bell and staggered up the stairs behind enormous bunches or boxes of flowers. The drawing room was filled with people talking Spanish or French or, occasionally, English, and drinking the pale sherry that Marya had rung up and ordered from a special shop in, appropriately enough, Swallow Street. Outside in Stacey Square, the usual row of modest little cars had been ousted by long, gleaming, expensive sports models.

Marya did not trouble about introductions; Chess and I came home from work and chatted to Carloses and Miguels and Tomasins without any hope of sorting them out. The older men were gradually weeded out and only the young ones remained. It was all very gay, but it was also noisy, and Mrs. Flower made frequent trips upstairs in order to complain.

I enjoyed it all very much, but—as I pointed out to Chess after a time—it involved us in a certain amount of expense.

"Can't you just enjoy it?" she asked. "When you think of the way you and I sat here for a whole month, not seeing a soul—"

"In about a week," I told her, "there'll be another month's rent due."

We had paid the last demand simply by scraping up every penny we could lay our hands on. I had exhausted my credit, Chess had used a birthday cheque that arrived too early, and Marya contributed a very small sum she remembered having left in a London bank.

"Don't worry until it comes," said Chess. "We paid it before and we can pay it again."

"Look," I said, and put before her a sheaf of bills.

They were not large, but size, after all, is relative; to us, they looked terrifying. There were bills for sherry, for olives and for cocktail biscuits, for more sherry and more olives.

"These are all Marya's," said Chess, after studying them

for a time.

"You and I have had our share of them," I pointed out.

Chess sat down slowly.

"Marya'll find the money," she said. " She says she hasn't got any, but look what she's managed to squeeze out of her father's friends since she came here."

"And look what she's spent it on," I said.

Looking had been a pleasure. Instead of paying her share of the general expenses, Marya had bought clothes. Beautiful, breath-taking clothes. Sitting on our beds when we came home from work, Chess and I had watched her laying them out for our inspection, and then putting them on for our approval. We had been envious, but appreciative; not once had one of us thought of so mundane a thing as a rent bill.

"We'll have to talk to Marya," said Chess.

We talked to her. As usual, she listened and thought about something else.

"It is not fair," she said, when I had painted a gloomy picture of our finances, "that I only should have my friends here all the time. Why do not all your friends come too?"

"We haven't many friends in London," I said. "Nobody we really like."

Marya looked from one to the other and frowned in bewilderment.

"But . . . one has a mother who is famous, and one has a father who is noble; with these, you have no interesting friends? "

"We're out of touch," explained Chess. " At least, I am. I've been living off the map, stuck down in Bath, meeting old ladies. And Denny never sees much of her mother."

"But your men friends—you must have men friends?" insisted Marya.

"We're engaged," I reminded her.

"But that is nonsense!" Her voice was louder than ever. "Your fiancés, who are so far away—do they expect that you see no other men?"

"They do expect," said Chess.

"Then they are stupid," said Marya contemptuously. "They are idiots. It is not for making love, you understand? It is only that a woman must go out. After all, you must lunch, no? You must dine, you must go to the theatre. Why should these fiancés fear anything? With girls like us, they know that there is no danger that we shall ever sleep with somebody."

This was sweeping, but in substance true. Differing greatly as we did in some respects, on this point the three of us were in complete agreement. Free love, we considered, was devised by men for men, while marriage was a splendid institution offering obvious advantages for women. We knew girls who seemed to get an invigorating sense of freedom as they leapt from one gentleman friend's bed to the next; we were not greatly concerned with the morals of the situation, but we felt that they were doing their sex a great disservice.

Chess, Marya and I had the same simple goal: love, courtship and marriage, in that order. No wedding, no bedding. As for the view that a lack of sex adventure would lead to Frustration with a capital F, or that Fulfilment (another capital) could be attained only in the narrow circle of a man's embrace—all that, we felt, was simply more male propaganda. We didn't exactly air these opinions, but we held them and we stuck to them.

"But your men friends," went on Marya, who was noted for persistence. "Where are they?"

There was a pause.

"Once you're engaged," Chess told her at last, "men seem to melt away."

"This," said Marya, "I do not understand."

"This I do not understand either," said Chess. "But it's true. Even before I was engaged, there wasn't what you'd call a queue. At the few parties I went to, I'd catch sight of a man or two, but they were all railed off behind possessive females."

"Then how," enquired Marya, "did you meet your fiancé?"

"I came up to the dentist in London and I met him— my fiancé, not the dentist—in the Underground. I knocked his briefcase out of his hand and right down the escalator, absolutely by mistake, and we went on from there."

We all gazed thoughtfully at the photograph on the table by Chess's bed.

"He looks interesting," said Marya, "but he is not here and you cannot stay at home all the time. I will get some men for you. And for you too, Denny."

"We don't want men; we want money," I said. "That pile of bills is for entertaining all those people. We can't keep it up."

"But when I came," said Marya, "you made up some little sums to show what we would spend on everything."

"We budgeted, yes. But we haven't kept to the budget."

"Even with you and Chess having a salary from your work, there is not enough?"

"Our salaries," I explained, "added to what I get from my father, pay for about three-quarters of our total expenses; seven-eighths, perhaps. Since you came, we've had a lot of fun and we're glad you're here and we love having you, but you haven't actually laid much money on the table, and until you do, we're going to go on being insolvent."

"If you asked your employers to give you more money—" began Marya.

"—we'd be out of jobs," finished Chess. "Denny might be able to earn more because she can write and type decent English, but what can I do? I'm the unemployable type; I can't do anything. Except work in Mrs. Flower's coffee bar."

"I would like to help you," said Marya, "but until my father is no longer angry, how can I get any money? He has told his friends not to help me."

"Then you'll have to work," said Chess.

"Work?" Marya's mouth opened slowly and stayed open.

"You needn't bother about learning how to type," I said. "The sort of job you could do would be selling dresses in one of those exclusive *boutiques."*

"Or you could try that travel firm I worked for," suggested Chess. "They threw me out after two days, but perhaps you know the difference between the Rhine and the Rhône; in case you don't, one wears a hat and the other doesn't."

"You can go and see the employment agency that fixed us up," I told Marya. "They might have something for you."

They placed her in a hat shop in Knightsbridge. Her job wasn't to sell hats; all she had to do was put them on. The sales must have gone up two hundred per cent—and with admirable foresight, I had told Marya to settle for a low salary and high commission.

After this, we settled down, and we felt that life was very pleasant. It was certainly harmonious—chiefly, I suppose, because three years together in one bedroom at Madame Narvik's had given us a fairly comprehensive knowledge of one another. I knew that Marya was lazy, rather stupid, and incapable of giving the least attention to any matter, however urgent, until she had satisfied herself that her hair, her dress and makeup were perfect to the last detail. I knew that Chess, who looked so much less intelligent than Marya, was much more so. I knew that Marya, who looked so warm and passionate, had less real interest in men than the comparatively cool-looking Chess. Neither of them was much help as far as housework went, but Marya, who loved clothes as some people love flowers, could not see them ill-used, and kept hers and ours pressed and tidy. Chess had an almost Moorish love of water, and liked nothing better than splashing at the sink; she would wash up without complaint, and as she lived on raw vegetables and salads, she was willing to prepare them for us all.

By degrees, we fell into a routine. Marya was always up first; lazy though she was, she could not bear to hurry her dressing and making-up. I was next out of bed, and I made the coffee. None of us ate breakfast, unless you counted Chess's yeast pills. I had to travel to the City, so I went off before the other two—but I was always home first, for Chess worked late at the coffee bar and Marya rarely came straight home; there was always a man eager to call for her and to drive her somewhere for drinks or for dinner.

It was not only in the evenings that she went out; there was a good deal going on in London, and the hat shop learned that she was subject to frequent headaches. As she was a Catholic and liked to keep her slate clean, it was left to Chess and to myself to telephone her excuses and make them sound convincing. While we were telephoning, Marya attended the Trooping of the Colour and similar picturesque functions, went to Ascot, and watched cricket and tennis, though her pleasure while watching the finals on the Centre Court at Wimbledon was slightly marred by the discovery that the manager of the hat shop was sitting just behind her.

Chess and I could live without tennis or cricket, but we both liked racing; as circumstances did not permit us to attend meetings, we laid bets on the stick-pin method, or put a shilling or two on our favourite jockey. Our modest bets were taken by Joe, delivery man at Preston's, the nearby grocer's shop at which we now dealt regularly. Mr. and Mrs. Preston, fat and good-natured, had taken us under their wing, and learning that none of us was in the house during the day to take in parcels, now sent our grocery orders to us after the shop had closed. They were brought by their son Basil or by their nephew Joe; Basil, gloomy and reserved, would do nothing but hand in the parcels from the delivery van and drive away, but Joe, cheerful and expansive, carried the things up to the kitchen, collected the empty bottles, helped us to empty the garbage and took it downstairs with him on his-way out. He also acted as waiter when Marya gave a party, and stayed on afterwards to wash the glasses; one way and another, we found him extremely useful.

If we wanted anything done in the flat, we asked Mr. Flower. Or rather, we asked Mrs. Flower and she ordered her husband to do it. She treated him, we thought, like a serf, but he never showed any resentment. Chess said that he gave the flat all the affection his wife had no use for; certainly he never looked happier than when he was attending to small repairs or putting touches of paint here and there in the flats.

We tried to get him to make the balcony safe; the evenings were getting warmer and we longed to sit outside when we came back from work—but Mr. Flower said that it was a builder's job, and told us regretfully that we could not use the balcony yet. Marya's job at the hat shop gradually reduced the number of guests at the flat; people who wanted to see her, saw her at work and I dare say bought hats in the intervals of waiting for her. I was glad to return to comparative tranquillity, but Chess wasn't; she missed the visitors.

"Why can't she bring people home as she used to? " she asked, as she and I sat down to yet another salad supper-for-two.

"She does sometimes," I said.

"They only come to call for her; they don't stay," complained Chess. "The only time—"

"They're her friends and not yours," I pointed out.

"I don't want her friends; I just want the overflow," said Chess. "All those men, and not one for you or me. Water, water everywhere and not a drop of drink."

"*To* drink."

"Of or to, I'm getting parched," Chess said.

"Well, Stephen will be back from New York in four days, and then you won't need anybody else."

She looked at me.

"Won't I?"

There was a pause while I analysed the odd note in her voice.

"That's absurd," I said at last. "You're just being silly. Perhaps in a way we've been a bit jealous of Marya."

"Not you. Me."

"Well, it was lonely to have to sit and wait for Stephen to come back, but he'll soon be here and—"

"—and at this moment," took up Chess, "I feel I just don't care if he stays where he is. You know something, Denny? The chief reason I got engaged is because you did."

I stared at her, but I could find nothing to say.

"It's true," she said. "When you wrote to say you'd got engaged, I felt ... I felt desperate. I'd been longing for you to get back to England; I was . . . well, I was trapped down there at Bath just waiting for you to come back."

"But you—"

"And then you wrote to say you were engaged. You didn't say anything about a flat, or London, that first time. You just said you were engaged. And so I stopped saying No to Stephen and I said Yes."

"If I didn't know you, I might believe that," I said. "Knowing you, I'm quite certain that when you said you'd marry him, you were in love with him."

"Or persuaded myself that I was. At the time, it seemed the only thing to do. I'd thought of other things; I thought of doing just what we're doing now; sharing a flat with you or with somebody else and getting a job. But when I thought of jobs, I thought of jobs in offices, and I knew I wouldn't last a week in one. I wondered if I could get a job as a cook, but I didn't think anybody would care to live permanently on tossed salads, which is about the extent of my cooking. So when you wrote to say that you were engaged, I fell right into Stephen's arms. And now ... I wish I hadn't."

"When he gets back, you'll feel different," I said. "It isn't easy to feel sure of yourself while you're so far away."

"You mean you feel that too?" she asked.

"Now and then. But wait and see: once Stephen appears, everything will be all right."

"No, it won't," Chess said. "You know why? Because all my life I'm going to regret not having had a choice."

"A choice? You had a choice; you could say Yes or you could say No."

"To one man. What I wanted was just a little of what Marya gets all the time: a chance to select. A chance to choose between this man or that man. In the end, I'd probably have chosen Steve, but at least I would have been able to look back all my life and remember the hearts I'd broken."

"You want to break hearts?"

"Doesn't every woman? I don't want to hurt anybody. I don't want to send any man to his bureau drawer feeling for his revolver; all I want is—"

"—to screw men up to proposing, so's you can turn them down?"

Chess drew a long, deep breath.

"Yes," she said.

"And that doesn't hurt them?"

"Oh, good heavens, Denny, no ! There are ways and ways. If you go steady for ages and give a man the idea that you're serious and then send him away, that's cheating. But what are men *for* if it isn't to ... to pay homage? Men—males—are supposed to dance round the females, all dressed up, fighting for favours. The men strut, the women select; that's plain, basic, down-to-Mother Nature."

"That might—"

"All this manoeuvring that women have to do nowadays to get a man . . . it's against nature," Chess said broodingly. "My nature, anyhow."

"But marriage—"

"Marriage is something else. Marriage, and I believe in it, is something that came with civilisation; you have children and you bring them up to be good citizens, and you cherish your husband, and that's fine. But there's nothing *basic* about it. It's just your intelligence telling you that it's the best thing in the long run. Deep down in every woman, Denny, I'm certain, is this feeling I've got now: the feeling that Nature meant women to *select* their mates. But how do you select if there's nothing to select *from*? All I wanted was a choice. If I'd had that, I would have settled down happily for the rest of my life. I think that most contented women—the women who are secure in their minds for ever and ever, whether they're married or whether they're not—are the ones who once in their lives—just once—had the privilege of choosing a whole man and who elected to have just his scalp. Selection— rejection. It's a woman's due, Denny, and to hell with having to take what comes."

She stopped for breath and there was silence. After waiting to see if she was going to give way to another outburst, I left her brooding, and cleared the table and carried the things into the kitchen and washed them up. It was a good thing, I thought, that Stephen was coming back to cure Chess's restlessness. It was easy to understand her reaction; it wasn't easy to watch Marya with her string of men and go on refusing to go out with any of them. We had sometimes gone out in parties, but this, we had found, usually meant coming home in pairs, and neither Chess nor I had Marya's experience in killing without wounding. While admiring the ability of Latin-American escorts to drive with one hand and make love with the other, we had discovered that it was better to forgo inviting invitations. So we had stayed at home, and Chess had of course found it dull—but soon Stephen would be back and all would be well.

Stephen returned on Thursday afternoon—and on Thursday evening, Uncle Philip came back to England and made his way to the flat.

We were all glad to see him. He had always been father and mother to me, and Chess and Marya had seen a good deal of him during our stay at Madame Narvik's, and they had become fond of him. He talked to Marya and myself for a time, and then two young men called for her, arriving at the same moment as Chess and Stephen.

I looked at Stephen, and liked what I saw. He was a short, powerful-looking young man with a quiet manner. It was difficult to talk to him, as Marya's friends monopolised the conversation, but I got a general impression of strength and dependability, and thought that Chess had done well.

Then they all went away, and Uncle Philip and I were left alone.

"Where do you want to dine?" he asked me.

"Here. Will you eat cheese and salad?"

"I'd far rather not," he said. "There's a little place called the Rivoli that—"

"We can talk so much better here. I've got heaps and heaps to tell you. You've never been away so long, and it's all been piling up."

"Very well; we shall talk here and eat somewhere else," he said.

He sat down and I sat at his feet and subjected him to a long survey. I was always frightened he would change in some way, but he never did, and now he looked just as usual: long and thin and dark, with a tropical suntan from his visits to the Far East; grey eyes and grey hair; quiet voice and quiet manner and a quiet, teasing humour I loved.

From my earliest years, he had always been just where I wanted him to be; he might go off on long journeys, but he seemed to appear by magic whenever I needed him. He was my mother's only close relation and he treated her with calm, brotherly affection and attended all her weddings and said nice things to me about her husbands. Without Uncle Philip, I don't know how things would have worked out, but he had been there always, his composed, fatherly presence giving us all a sort of dignity we wouldn't otherwise have had. Throughout my schooldays, he had come, with or without my mother, to half-terms and Speech days, and had never let me spend the holidays alone.

He had never married; he knew a great many people in London, but he disliked parties, and for the most part lived quietly at his Club.

I was always especially glad to see him when he came back from his business travels; now I talked and talked and talked, and he listened without interruption. I told him about the flat and the Flowers, Mr. and Mrs.; I told him about our jobs and our way of life; I sketched in gloomy Basil and jolly Joe and the coffee bar and the hat shop and my job in the City. Uncle Philip listened and, I knew, enjoyed listening.

"I see," he said at last, when I had stopped talking. "Well, it all sounds very satisfactory. Except that Marya seems to be the only one having a gay time."

"Yes." I grinned at him. "But Stephen's back now, and Chess—"

"Does Chess still have theories?"

"Yes. Quite sound ones, I think. Now Stephen's back, she'll be able to tell them to him. Did you like him?"

"He seemed a very nice young man. But I'd be a good deal more interested to hear about your own. Why," he enquired, "did you become engaged without giving me a chance to look him over?"

"I ... It all happened rather suddenly," I said.

"So I gathered. You met him when you were in Rome and he turned out to be the brother of one of the girls you had shared a flat with in London. What else?"

"He went to Rome for his firm, and when he'd finished the job there, he had to go out to Malaya."

"And in between, he fell in love with you?"

"Yes. There wasn't much time to—"

"There was time for you to fall in love too?"

"I . . . Yes," I said.

He turned my face so that he could look down at it. For a little while, he just looked. Then:

"You're quite sure he's what you want?" he asked. I hesitated. I thought of Chess, who had not been sure, but who now had Stephen beside her to reassure her.

"Quite sure," I said. "At least . . ."

"At least?"

"When he went away, I was pretty sure," I said at last. "He gave me a little time to think about it, and I thought about it, and . . . and we got on very well, and . . . and it'll be all right."

Uncle Philip released my chin and lit a cigarette and leaned back in his chair.

"And so that covers everything," he said. "The flat, the three girls in it and their young men. Perfection everywhere, but I gather not enough money."

"Not nearly enough."

"And you still won't take any from me?"

I wriggled round to stare up at him.

"You *do* understand, don't you?" I said.

"I try to. You won't take it from your mother because she—"

"—because she won't give me her own."

"Because she feels that by doing so, she would drive a wedge between you and the man she hopes you'll learn to look on as a father."

"The man? The men."

There was a short silence.

"I saw her last week," he said after a time.

"In the villa?"

"No. In Paris."

"I see. They've parted, I suppose?"

"Yes."

"Is there anybody else?"

"No."

"There will be," I said.

Uncle Philip rose and put out his cigarette.

"Time to go and dine," he said. "Will you ring up for a

taxi?"

I rang up, and we went to the Rivoli, which is one of the places Uncle Philip seems to find by a sort of instinct. Small, quiet and exceedingly select, with food that's something to dream about. He ordered for himself, ordered, after some argument, for me, and then sat lost behind the wine list. When he emerged, he smiled at me.

"Nice to have you again," he said. "You're looking very pretty."

"Thank you. You might tell that to a few more of Marya's friends. Some of them glance away from her; most of them don't."

"You're too close to the blinding light. They can't see you very well."

"We worked that out, Chess and I, for our own comfort," I told him. "How was my mother?"

"Thank you for enquiring," he said gravely. "She, too, was looking very pretty."

"I'm glad," I said.

Uncle Philip, who wasn't having soup, watched me as I tried the kind he had recommended for me.

"Nice?" he asked.

"Simply wonderful."

"Perhaps it'll put some flesh on your bones. Speaking of flesh," he went on casually, "I saw your father too. He'd put on weight. Too much weight, as I told him."

I put down my spoon.

"Where?" I asked.

"Round the middle, mostly. Developed a bit of a paunch, and—"

"Where," I broke in, "did you see him?"

"In Singapore. If I'd known your young man was to be there too, I would have—"

"Did he ask about me?"

"Your young man?"

I took a deep breath.

"You want me to throw this soup at you?"

"I'd rather you didn't."

"Then: did my father mention me?"

"We talked of nothing else," said Uncle Philip, " for three hours."

I thought this over.

"Then what?" I asked.

"Then he drove me to the airport."

"And—?"

"One of the things he brought up was the question of the allowance he makes you."

"And that," I said slowly, "is something that you could have made him do years and years ago."

"I could have; true. Finish your soup; I'm hungry."

I finished it. "Why—" I began, but Uncle Philip raised a

hand and stopped me.

"Talking," he said, "should be a two-way track. You talked at the flat; forty minutes non-stop. Now it's my turn."

"Go ahead," I invited.

"Very well. First," he said, "I wish you were my daughter instead of my niece."

"Me too," I said.

"Thank you. But for a number of years—twenty- four to be exact—I've tried to be a father to you. And for about thirteen of those years, I've tried to be a mother, too."

"Thank *you"* I said. "You make a good job of it."

"Your mother," he said, "wants you to live with her."

I spoke without the slightest hesitation.

"The answer is no," I said.

There was a pause.

"You could think about it," suggested Uncle Philip after a time.

"I did that," I told him. "I did that after her last divorce but one. She was alone, and I was old enough to wonder whether perhaps the reason for all the husbands was in some way for my sake. To fill a gap, or something. But I was wrong. And I learned something else, too: she didn't want me. At least, she didn't want only me. You know, and I know, that she has to have husbands. That's better than Marya's father, who doesn't bother to get married to his lady friends, but it isn't my idea of a quiet, steady home life. In some ways, I like my mother. In some ways, I don't."

"She has made a success of her work," pointed out Uncle Philip. "And she has never let the slightest breath of scandal touch her—or touch you. She's beautiful, she's elegant; her husbands, all four of them, have been decent men, and all of them have tried to make you like them."

"I did like them."

"But you wouldn't take anything—"

"No. Neither would anybody else have done. My mother wanted them to provide for me, because that way, we'd look like a real family."

"What was wrong with that?"

"Children aren't the fools people take them for. One of the first things I discovered was that the home-life picture was just a backcloth; nothing more. My mother had it painted, and it looked nice and real—a long way off. She played a scene against it, and then the scene was over and the scenery had to be changed. When I got to an age at which I could choose, I wouldn't have minded taking anything—money, a home, affection—from a stepfather. What I couldn't have done, and can't do and won't ever do, is adopt one stranger after another as a father and a provider and a benefactor. I'd rather keep myself."

I stopped—hopefully. This was the point at which, I felt, Uncle Philip might well revert to the subject of the allowance my father gave me. But he said nothing; he sat for some time looking thoughtful and then the *maître d' hôtel* came up and we got into a discussion about *crêpes suzettes;* they were as light as air, and so was our conversation for the rest of dinner.

Uncle Philip took me up to the flat, but didn't stay; he said good night and kissed me and went away, leaving me happy and drowsy and relaxed, as I always was after he'd taken me out.

I changed into a housecoat and tidied up the drawing room; I was just going across the landing to run my bath when the buzzer buzzed.

I thought it must be Uncle Philip, and looked over my shoulder into the drawing room to see what he'd left behind—and then I remembered that he was a man who seldom forgot anything. Chess, I thought, might have forgotten her key. I went downstairs and opened the front door.

It wasn't Chess. A very tall, very thin man of about thirty was standing on the doorstep. He was wearing a dinner jacket and carrying a long sheaf of flowers, and as the door opened, he gave a slight bow.

"I've called for Miss Annuzio," he said.

He took a step forward, half-expecting me to stand aside and let him in, but I didn't move.

"I'm sorry," I said. "Marya's out."

He smiled; it was a happy smile, wide and untroubled. He wore glasses with the largest rims I'd ever seen; they looked as big as portholes.

"She'll be back," he said. "I'm taking her to a nightclub."

"Oh!" I felt relieved; it would have been terrible to have brought those flowers—red roses, I saw—for nothing. Why, I wondered fleetingly, didn't Marya's admirers sometimes bring fruit instead of flowers? It would have saved us a lot of money. "In that case, there's been a slight mistake; she must have arranged to meet you there."

Still happy, he shook his head.

"Mm-Mm," he murmured negatively. "She arranged to meet me here."

"But she went out to dinner," I said, "and told me that she was going on to a night-club. The Caribbean."

There was a pause, during which I sensed that whatever night-club Portholes had had in mind, it hadn't been the Caribbean.

"I'm sorry," I said again, and looked at the flowers. "Shall I . . . would you like me to take them and put them in water for her?"

"A nice thought." His accent was transatlantic; not strongly, but unmistakably. He handed over the flowers. Then:

"Perhaps I could come up and wait?" he suggested.

I spoke more coolly.

"She won't be back until two or three in the morning," I said.

"I could read a book."

"I'm afraid—"

"I wouldn't disturb you at all; you could go on with whatever it was you were going to do," he said.

"I was going to have a bath and go to bed," I told him, and now I sounded frosty. "It's nearly half past eleven."

"For a night, that's young," he said.

He looked at the flowers; for a moment I thought he was going to take them back again.

"I'll tell Marya that you called," I said.

"Do that," he said. "And tell her I'll call again."

I began to close the door; the light was dim and grew dimmer as I shut him out; the portholes gleamed and looked larger than ever.

"I could take a nap on the sofa until she came back," he said.

"I'm sorry," I said distantly.

"You're Denny, aren't you?"

I wondered how he knew, but I didn't ask.

"Yes," I said. "And now, if you'll excuse me—"

"Oh. Well, au revoir," he said.

"Good-bye," I answered.

Which, in the light of later events, was very, very funny.

Chapter Three

A few days later, Chess and I noticed something unusual: Marya had gone out several times with the same man.

Unusual isn't quite the word. This was something extraordinary; it was, in fact, a phenomenon.

Marya didn't make engagements in the way most sought-after girls did. She had no little diary full of scribbles denoting dates, and she didn't dash breathlessly from one engagement to the next, intermittently trying to fit in yet one more party between many others. On the contrary, she made no engagements at all, and there was no day on which she could have said, on leaving the hat shop, exactly what she was going to do that evening.

This casual behaviour sent her friends into a frenzy, but it was in keeping with her unhurried way of life. She was moody, and she liked to suit the man and the place to the mood. Many moods, many men—and so when she went out four times in one week with a man called Laurence Gale, Chess and I took uneasy note of the fact. And having taken note, we came to the conclusion that if she was going to single one man out from the rest, she could hardly have picked on a poorer specimen.

Laurence Gale was an Englishman whose parents lived in Chile; he had spent as much time there as in England, and seemed to have become a sort of hybrid; his English—when he spoke English—was impeccable, but his clothes and his manners were modelled on what Chess and I supposed he supposed was the most irresistible Chilean model. He was tall and very dark and rather cadaverous and looked haunted; if you liked that kind of thing, Chess said, he certainly had it. He was well known in debonair circles, and his name appeared frequently in the gossip columns.

"I would have thought," Chess said, "that she'd have had better taste. It must have been the fancy dress that did it."

I agreed with this. He had called to take Marya to a fancy dress dance, and was dressed as a matador. He looked sensational, and Manolete must have stirred uneasily in his grave.

"The funny thing," went on Chess, "is that none of those other men of hers ever took their eyes off her— but this one spreads himself thinly. He must have taken out every attractive girl in town, in his time. Except you and me."

"Well, if she likes him, she likes him," was all I could find to say.

"I think he's terrible. I'd much rather have seen her with Portholes," said Chess. "Speaking of Portholes, why doesn't he give up?"

I couldn't tell her. Portholes was showing amazing stamina. Marya scarcely remembered having met him; she recalled only that it was at a riverside party at a house in Chiswick—

but every evening at about seven, the buzzer went, and there he was on the doorstep, with the same half-shy, half-happy smile, the same easy, relaxed manner, the same cairn disregard of mild or strong hints. He came upstairs, joined the group in the drawing room, asked Marya casually how she felt about going out, bowed at her equally casual refusal and opened the door for her as she went out with Laurence Gale. Other men, perhaps sensing Laurence's triumph, had begun to drop away, but Portholes arrived without fail every evening, at first with flowers, then with fruit and at last with wine. If a man walks in with a bottle of wine, it's difficult to snatch it from him and lock it in the cellar for another occasion; trapped, Chess and I asked him to stay to supper. He accepted without hesitation, helped Stephen to lay the table, showed us a new way of dressing salad and throughout the meal talked non-stop about Marya. He told us that his name was Fergus Maitland, and followed this up by a suggestion that we should go on calling him Portholes.

"How did he know we did?" Chess asked me later.

"Marya must have told him—or he overheard. You can hear a lot as you come up the stairs, if the kitchen or the drawing room doors are open. Are we stuck with him, do you think, for ever?"

It looked so much like it that Chess appealed to Marya.

"If you're never going out with him," she said, "why don't you tell him it's no use? Steve's getting tired of staying in every evening so's not to leave Denny marooned with him."

"I've told you," I said. "You and Stephen can go out; I can deal with this Maitland."

So on the following evening, they all went out and I was left for the first time alone with the limpet. I thought that the best thing, the kindest thing, would be a sort of gentle frankness, so as soon as the front door had closed, I began to be gently frank.

"I'm afraid," I said, "you've been having rather a difficult time, but—"

"I'm having a wonderful time," he said. " All this charming hospitality."

"—but I've known Marya for a long time and—"

"I wouldn't have said," he remarked, on his way round emptying small ash trays into one very large one, "that she would have wasted time on a chap like Gale. Dead loss, I'd say, from a woman's point of view."

"Perhaps," I agreed. " But this is the first time that Marya has ever—"

"—covered the same ground more than once? It's interesting," he said, "but not, I think, permanent."

He was collecting the empty sherry glasses and putting them on a tray; he put the large, now full ash tray beside them, saw a smudge of ash on the sofa, and proceeded to beat it out; Mr. Flower himself couldn't have shown more solicitude for the appearance of the room.

"What I'm trying to say, as kindly as possible," I said, "is that as far as you're concerned—"

"No go?" He stepped back to peer at the sofa and seemed satisfied with his work; picking up the tray, he carried it to the door and then paused. "You mean she'll never look at me? Possibly not; possibly not. But you know, it occurs to me that I'm not the type of man to kill at a blow, like Gale. I'm roughly the type, I'd say, who'd grow on a woman. She sees me, she gets used to seeing me; I become part of the scene."

"Yes, but—"

"And when you've got used to seeing something around, if it's not there, you miss it."

I tried to find a polite way of asking him how soon we should have the pleasure of missing him, but he had vanished towards the kitchen. I followed him, to see him stacking the glasses beside the sink.

"Thank you," I said. "Just leave them, will you? I'll deal with them when you've gone."

"I can't leave you to wash up all alone," he said. "Is this"—his eyes fell on the preparations for my supper—"all you're going to eat?"

"Yes."

"Slimming? You don't look—"

"I don't," I said, " care for a heavy meal at night."

"Cream soup, *wiener schnitzel* and *crepes suzettes,"* he said.

I stared at him.

"How do you—"

"I was at the table behind the potted palm. If I'd known you were a friend of Marya's, I would have— Ah!"

He had seen, in an open cupboard, our stores. They consisted of an opened packet of brown sugar, a tin of wheaten biscuits, some cheese, two eggs and a tin of tuna fish.

"Do you ever," he asked, picking up the tin, "eat this the right way?"

"We—"

"Could I use it?"

"I think," I said, "it would be much better if you went away and dined properly."

"Marya," he said, "might come back early, and then I could see her. Tin opener?"

I handed him one; he helped himself to an onion, a lemon and some parsley, and took the chopping board off its hook.

"Fish in a bowl—so," he said. "Onion chopped very finely; mix with fish—so. Parsley also chopped— so. Mix with fish and onions—so. Lemon juice over all, and toss. I don't," he said, proceeding to gather the knives and forks from the drawer, "care for tinned food, but if you must use it, this is a better way than most."

There seemed nothing to say. Saying nothing, I laid the table in the drawing room and got out a clean table napkin for him.

"You're Irish?" he asked, as he pulled out my chair for

me.

"Yes."

"North? South?"

"County Kerry."

"You don't look or sound Irish," he commented, heaping salad on to my plate.

"You don't look or sound particularly English."

"These glasses?" He adjusted them.

"And your American accent."

"Canadian," he corrected. " I was one of those children whose parents shipped them off to Canada when the Nazis were preparing to swim the English Channel. I stayed out there when the War ended, and the accent stayed with me.—You never, with so famous a mother, wanted to go on the stage?"

"No."

"Is your father dead, like mine?"

"No."

"I'm sorry," he said, and I knew what he meant. "When does your fiancé get back to England?"

"Not for two years."

"Two years," he commented, " is quite a slice out of a girl's life. Two years without a sight of the man —"

"He doesn't share your views about the necessity of being round all the time," I said. "He believes, as I do, that if you really want something, you can wait for it and—"

"Patience," he said, reaching for some more fish, "is a hungry virtue. You have to feed it. You have to keep on feeding it. You can either feed it from day to day, as I'm doing, with the sight and the sound of the loved one, or you can feed it from a rich store of beautiful memories." He peered through the portholes. "You have a rich store of beautiful memories?"

"Yes," I lied.

"You knew him for a long time before you became engaged to him?"

"I . . . Not very long. There's some more wine, if you'd care for some."

"No, thank you. How long, exactly?"

"Two months."

"You can fit a lot into two months," he said reflectively. "But enough to feed Patience for two long years?"

He seemed to ponder, and I remembered that they had been cold, wet months and Rome had been grey and cheerless and my memories were mostly of noisy restaurants or crowded bars. I wouldn't have said there was a rich storehouse—but there was a promise made, and the hope of happiness to come.

When Chess and Stephen came back, Portholes was still there, and I was surprised to find that it was close on midnight. He stayed on for a drink with Stephen, and then went away, asking us to give Marya his fondest love.

"Tell her," he said, as he closed the door behind him, "that I'll look in to see her tomorrow."

We heard the front door close.

"Well!" Chess drew a long breath. "How's that for hope eternal?"

"Odd chap," remarked Stephen.

He was very odd compared with Stephen, who looked every psychologist's dream of the perfectly co-ordinated man. His eyes were clear and intent until he looked at Chess, when they became remote and dreamy. He looked simple, forthright and desperately in love; I thought Chess was lucky to have got him.

But Chess, unfortunately, didn't seem to think so. Since his return, she had been behaving in a way quite unlike her usual sensible self, and she spoke to Stephen sometimes in a voice that—for Chess—was almost sharp. To my relief, he didn't appear to notice. But on the afternoon following my tête-à-tête with Portholes, she rang me up at my office.

"Can you hear me?" she asked.

"Of course I can hear you."

"I didn't want to talk too loudly. It's about Stephen."

"What about Stephen?"

"When you get home, will you ring him and tell him I'm in bed with a headache, or something?"

"If you're in bed with a headache, of course I will."

"Well, I won't be," said Chess irritably. "But I don't want to see him."

"You don't—"

" I want a break. I want a bit of time away from him. But when I suggested it to him, he blew up."

"Well, you—"

"This evening," she said, "I'm going out with Edward."

I drew a long, bewildered breath.

"Who in the world," I asked, "is Edward?"

"Edward Royle. You don't know him, but he's been coming to the coffee bar for ages and trying to get me to go out with him. I've always said No—and now I've said Yes. And I'm going, so don't waste time arguing."

"I think you're crazy," I said.

"I think I'm crazy, too," Chess said. "Not to have done it before."

She didn't come home that evening. Stephen arrived looking puzzled and depressed; she had rung him up and told him, I gathered, more or less what she had told me. His sole reason for coming in spite of this, he said, was to see whether she meant it. Apparently she did; he sat with Marya and Portholes and myself until about half past eight, and then got up and took his leave.

Marya and I tried, in our different ways, to reason with him.

"I have told you and told you, Stephen," said Marya, "that this Edward is very dull. I have met him, and I know that he thinks of one thing only: his horses. Polo, polo, polo. After one evening with him, Chess will feel like a horse. If you will be patient—"

But Stephen was out of the door. I followed him down the stairs; it was hard work keeping up with him, and I hated the idea of trying to keep him when he didn't want to stay, but I liked him and I didn't want Chess to lose him.

"Look, Stephen—"

"If she thinks I'm a damned jellyfish, like that fellow Maitland, sitting up there waiting for Marya to find out he's alive, then she's damned well mistaken," he said. "You can tell her so."

"But Stephen, it's just that she—"

"She's following the example of your little pet, Marya, and trying to run a string of men all at the same time. If Chess does that, she'll run into trouble. Marya's a tough proposition; Chess isn't."

"There's nothing wrong with Marya," I said.

"No?" He stopped at the bottom of the stairs to glare at me angrily over his shoulder. "No?"

"No," I said.

Upon this brilliant exchange, the door banged. Marya went out shortly afterwards with Laurence Gale, and Portholes and I were left. I came out of a troubled day-dream to find him in the kitchen preparing supper. Smoked salmon and cold chicken; he had brought it with him and all we had to do was eat it. But I didn't feel like eating.

"A quarrel," Portholes reminded me, "can be very stimulating."

"Can it?"

"And a man like Stephen can—"

"A man like Stephen is hard to come by," I said angrily, "and she shouldn't play the fool and risk losing him. All this yes-ing and no-ing . . . what's got into her?"

"The Spring?" he suggested mildly.

"She used to have a lot of sense."

"She still has. If she doesn't look round a little, how will she know what she really wants?"

This was so like Chess's own theory that I had nothing to say. When I next saw Uncle Philip, he told me, as Portholes had done, that I was taking the matter far too seriously.

"Let her take a look round," he advised. "If there's enough between her and Stephen, they'll come together some time. Why," he enquired casually, "don't you take a look round yourself?"

"Because I'm engaged, that's why."

"Surely he won't expect you to—"

"—to sit around for two years without seeing another man? I don't suppose so. On the other hand, it wouldn't be much fun for him to read letters from me full of accounts of which night-club I'd been frequenting, and with which escort. Though it would," I acknowledged unwillingly, "make writing a good deal easier."

Uncle Philip's eyebrows went up.

"But you're an excellent letter writer!"

"To you. When I write to you, I can just ramble on; I can talk of people we both know, and remind you of . . ." I stopped. *A rich store of beautiful memories.*

Uncle Philip was watching me.

"Well?" he asked at last.

"Nothing. Just something I remembered."

He lit a cigarette before he spoke again. Then: "You're quite sure, Denny, I suppose?"

"About my engagement? I told you: yes. But I'm not going to pretend that we say much in our letters. We don't. I sit down with a writing pad in front of me, and mostly, nothing comes. I put down everything I do, and it reads like a time table: dead."

"And his letters?"

"The same. Only more so, because he writes less often. Sometimes I don't hear for two or three weeks. Then he tells me what he's been doing, and every name he mentions means exactly nothing; like me, he can't fall back on reminiscences or on gossip about people we both know, because we never did know the same people—with the exception of his sister."

"And you think you can go on saying nothing for two years?"

"It might die a natural death," I said, "but if it does, it'll be a pity, because there must have been a moment —mustn't there?—when we were both sure?"

"I suppose so," he agreed gently. "But don't blame Chess too much. Let her be. Let her sort it out with Stephen."

"You didn't see him last night. He looked deadly. *He* won't sit around waiting."

"Is that all that's worrying you?"

"No. This Laurie Gale's on my mind too. He doesn't take out girls for nothing. Everybody knows his reputation: bed and bored. I can't bear to think of Marya—"

I stopped.

"Go on," invited Uncle Philip.

"She can do as she likes, I suppose," I said without conviction.

"Precisely. So can Chess. There's the bell."

It was the bell to mark the end of the intermission; we were at the theatre watching a very dull play: imitation Chekov. Afterwards, we went on to supper and I ate my way halfway through the menu and felt much better.

The waiter brought the bill, and I was going to apologise for its largeness when Uncle Philip looked up.

"I spoke to your mother yesterday," he said.

I stared at him.

"She's in London?" I asked.

"She was in Paris. She rang me late last night."

"To say what?"

"To tell me she was coming to London. The reason she rang me and not you was to talk to me about getting her a flat."

"She's got—"

I stopped. I had been about to say that she already had a perfectly good flat in Brook Street, but I remembered that it had belonged not to her but to my last stepfather.

"When is she coming?" I asked.

"Next week."

"So is Marya's father."

"I thought you told me that she'd quarrelled with him."

"She had. He's still furious, but I suppose he finds it difficult to get her attention all the way from South America. He's coming over—she thinks—to apply pressure."

"How do fathers do that nowadays?" Uncle Philip wanted to know. "I thought their days of influence were at an end."

"I think he'll use money."

"That, of course, was always a strong lever. Will he bribe her to go home?"

"Not exactly. But he can offer her a more comfortable flat—with himself in it."

"Will she go?"

I wasn't sure. I put the question to her that night. She got home just after Chess, and we all sat in the kitchen and drank coffee because we'd run out of malted milk.

"Go and live with him in another flat? No, I will not," she said. "I won't leave you and Chess."

"The faithful type," remarked Chess. "What kind of coffee is this?"

"The cheapest kind they sell," I told her. "The kind you bought is for millionaires—or for Marya when she goes back to her father."

"I shall not," declared Marya. "With you and Chess, I feel ... I feel like a ship with two good anchors."

"A couple of buoys would suit you better," said Chess flippantly.

"You think I am not serious? I am," Marya assured us earnestly. "Without you, I could not of course live like this, with no beauty to look at in the rooms, no comfort, not enough space; it would be impossible. But with you, it is like Madame Narvik's; it is not home, but it is like a sort of home. I like it."

"I like it too," said Chess. "But your father'll try to get you out of it, and Denny's mother is trying to get her out of it. They'll soon be in London—and just as soon as my parents get my letter telling them I've switched from Stephen to Edward, they'll be here too. That is, if they read between the lines and discover that they're losing a golden egg—or do I mean a golden goose? Doesn't matter; all that matters is that this place is soon going to look like the walls of Jericho."

"How?" enquired Marya.

"They walked round and round—I forget who," said Chess, "blowing trumpets, and the walls of Jericho fell down."

"Our parents are the trumpets?"

"And we're the walls," said Chess.

"Nobody can make us leave this flat if we don't want to,"

I pointed out. "We're keeping ourselves; we've got jobs, and we look solvent."

"Solvent?" enquired Marya.

"Able to be dissolved," explained Chess. "That's what we'll be if we're not careful."

"But soon we shall marry; so much is certain," said Marya. "Why should not my father leave me to be happy here until that time?"

"Because when you marry, it'll be too late," said Chess. "He wants you while he can get you. The fact that you'd rather live here won't—Gosh, what's the matter?"

The matter was that Marya had burst into tears.

When I cry, which is seldom, or when Chess cries, which is even less frequent, our faces get red and swollen, and we snuffle or sob. Marya's face merely crinkled, and then tears began to pour down her cheeks; she made no sound, but just sat there trying to brush away the tears with the back of her hand, like a child.

I got up and went into the bedroom and returned with a box of tissues, which I handed to her.

"What is it?" asked Chess. "I said something?"

"N-no. Nothing." There was an interval while Marya dried her tears. "But for you two, it is different; it is easy. For me, it is not so easy."

"What's not so easy?" I asked.

"Your parents—Chess's and yours—they were different,"

explained Marya. "They went away, or they married several times, and you do not owe them so very much. But my father . . . Always, he kept me with him. Other fathers like him, with business to look after in this, in that part of the world, other fathers left their children. But my father, never. When I was at Narvik's was the only time I was not with him. For the rest of my life, wherever he went, he took me. He took women, too, of course, because he said that he needed them—but he never forgot about me. He never left me. At night, wherever we were, my bedroom would have a door to his, and if I cried out or called to him, he would at once unlock his door and come to me. Always, I came first and his women came afterwards. He gave me everything that I wanted—except a home that was in one place. This he could not do, because he had to travel for his business. But always, he took me with him. Now ... I do not want to go with him any more."

"And so you've got a guilt complex," said Chess. "Well, that's something that doesn't keep Denny or myself awake at night."

"Why does he not understand that I wish to stay here?" asked Marya through a fresh downpour.

"Don't ask me how parents' minds work," said Chess. "I don't understand parents. All I know is that when I marry, I'm going to have a lot of children, not just one little misery. An only child has to shoulder all the parent trouble; five or six of them can spread the load. And I'm going to give my children a home. A home, if you want me to define it, is a place where you can keep your things while you're growing up. Your books, your toys, your treasures."

"Parents," I said, "seem to draw the booby prize whichever way you look at it. If they're bad parents, they lose their children. If they're good parents, self- sacrificing parents, they lose their children anyway. If all of us had had model parents, we'd still be sitting here swearing we wouldn't give up our freedom."

"I shall tell my father," declared Marya, "that I am going to stay here with you until we marry."

"And speaking of marrying," said Chess, "I hope you won't consider Laurie Gale."

Marya looked at us.

"Why do you both think that he is a bad man?" she asked.

"We don't think," said Chess. "You've only got to look at him. He's too transparent for words; you can see straight through him to the chaise-longue on the other side."

"That is what makes him harmless," said Marya. "And if you wish to know, I do not like this Edward Royle you are making so much fuss about."

"What's wrong with him?" asked Chess.

"He is nothing, nothing, nothing compared with Stephen," declared Marya. "If you do not wish to marry Stephen, that is your affair, but do not exchange him for a stupid man like Edward Royle."

"He's a good deal more exciting than Stephen, and more

interesting, and a whole lot better informed," said Chess. "When I've been out with Edward, I feel as though I'd had my battery re-charged; that was something I never experienced with Stephen."

Marya rose, shrugged and drew her dressing gown round her. It was flimsy and floating and it made the ones Chess and I were wearing look like something that a couple of orphans had grown out of.

"You should take my advice," she told Chess. "I know about men, and I tell you that you should forget about this Royle, and go back to Stephen."

"And I tell you," I said, putting out the light, "that you're both going to bed and we're all going to get some sleep. Good night."

Chapter Four

The next week was Parents' Week.

We had all met one another's parents, for they had come at one time or another to visit us at Madame Narvik's. Mr. Annuzio had been our first visitor, and he had taken the three of us away for a week-end: car to Capri, speed boat when we got there, and a hotel suite that must have cost a small fortune. He had the suite adjoining ours and we would probably have enjoyed his company if he hadn't brought along a little piece called Cleobelle. She was only about our age, but she hadn't wasted any time at places like Madame Narvik's. Before the week-end ended, she had flown at Marya—who deserved it—on the hotel terrace. Marya, the picture of cool dignity, waited her moment and side-stepped; Cleobelle hit the terrace and we three packed up and went back to Madame Narvik's, leaving Mr. Annuzio and Cleobelle discussing damage clauses. After that, his visits were confined to dropping in carrying enormous baskets of fruit, patting us all in a fatherly way, and departing.

Chess's parents came only once—to see, I think, what it was about the place that was costing the plebeian aunt so much. They didn't stay long, and by the time they left, Marya and I understood many things about Chess that hadn't been clear before.

Her parents had married late in life; the Countess was over forty when Chess, the only child, was born. Husband and wife were an ideally happy couple, but their affection, unfortunately, centered solely upon one another, and Chess had long ago given up trying to direct some of it towards herself. Her parents were kind, but it was clear even to casual observers that they had to make stern efforts in order to remember that they had a child. Madame Narvik was not a casual observer.

My mother came on several visits, and always created a sensation. We went out preceded and followed by newsmen and photographers and she made personal appearances here and there and gave all the girls her autograph. I think she always went away with a feeling of honest pleasure at having boosted my prestige, but it took me days to recover from the hotch-potch of feelings she'd left me with: embarrassment at the ballyhoo, guilt for not being more grateful, admiration for her beauty and hatred of the professional way in which she used it.

Now all the parents were converging upon us at once. Mr. Annuzio arrived first and made his way to the hat shop, to find his daughter entrenched behind a barricade of saleswomen, managers, manageresses and customers. Retreating, he rented a luxurious house and settled in it to embark upon a campaign of contrasts : Rutland Gate versus Stacey Square.

Next on the scene were Chess's parents. Their interest in

her engagement, at first slight, had taken a steep upward curve when they learned the satisfactory state of Stephen's finances. Chess's last letter had, as she anticipated, brought them hurrying home, for though Edward was extremely well-connected, his high-sounding title could not compensate the Earl and the Countess for the fact that he was also Edward the Impecunious. I would have liked to feel that their journey had been undertaken solely on Chess's behalf, but I knew that her interpretation of their solicitude was probably correct: they were coming to prevent, if possible, a rich son-in-law from slipping away from them. On their arrival, they settled themselves in the few rooms they kept furnished at their castle in Kent, and then sought out Stephen and tried to persuade him to make the first move towards a reconciliation. Stephen refused, which was just as well, since Chess had no desire to be reconciled. She had sent Stephen back his ring and she was, she said, going to marry Edward.

Finding Stephen stubborn, the Earl and Countess came to the flat and asked me down to Kent for the week-end—with a view, I knew, to pressing me to use my influence with Chess and make her see reason. I had to accept, but by a stroke of luck, Marya came in just as I did so; after a slight hesitation, the Countess felt herself obliged to extend the invitation to her.

"But I did not wish to go," Marya told me indignantly when they had gone away.

"Neither did I," I said. "But I'm glad you're coming; with you there, they won't be able to corner me all the time."

"If they say to me do I like Edward, I shall have to tell them no, and then Chess will be angry."

"You'll have to be tactful, that's all," I said. "And it isn't until the week-end after next; they may change their minds by that time."

And in the meantime, my mother came to London and we fell into our usual uneasy relationship.

We never quarrelled. She wasn't the quarrelling kind. She was invariably quiet, almost gentle, with a voice that was low and slightly husky; she wasn't thin, but she had a fragile look; people called her ethereal.

Usually, we spent the time together saying everything that didn't matter, and nothing that did; when the silences began to lengthen, she would get up and float away.

We had never spoken of my father. I discovered very early in life that it was useless to ask her for information about him; she never mentioned his name. Uncle Philip was not much more informative; he explained, when he thought I was old enough to understand, that no outsider could ever assess exactly what it was that had made a marriage go wrong. They had married, he said, and when I was fourteen months old, my father had left my mother, and the pair had not met since that day. That was as far as Uncle Philip ever went, and I can't tell when or how began the slow process by which I came to understand that there was more to the story than there appeared to be. The more I learned of my mother's character, the more surely I knew that the picture of her as a frail girl, a mother at nineteen, abandoned by her husband and left without a penny was a false one. I sensed other things, too; I came by degrees to see that Uncle Philip had no more illusions about my mother than I had—but he showed her unfailing kindness and courtesy and never discussed her, and I had learned to do the same.

This time things were easier, because she seldom saw me alone; when she called at the flat of an evening, Marya would go out with Laurie, Chess would go out with Edward—but always there would be left, anchored, immovable, Fergus Maitland.

I had got used to him. Having tried every way of making him see that he was wasting his time hanging round Marya, I gave up and decided to let him sit it out. I had grown so accustomed to his presence that I behaved, most of the time, as though he were not there. If I wanted to write letters, I wrote them, and he picked up a book and read; once I fell asleep doing the accounts, and he crept away.

"Why," my mother asked one evening when she and I were dining out with Uncle Philip, "does he come?"

I told her.

"Then why don't you go out every night?" she asked.

"Where to?"

"You could come and see me."

"I don't think that would move him. Whenever Uncle Philip takes me out, he stays away; next evening, he's back again."

"Then he must be interested in you and not in Marya."

"If he is, he shows it in a funny way," I said. "He talks about Marya, brings her presents and writes little notes and leaves them for her."

"Hasn't he got anything else to do? No other friends?"

"He's got a sister living down at Dorking. And an aunt somewhere."

"What does he do?"

"He's a barrister."

"And he is simply hanging round hoping that Marya will change her mind?"

"Yes."

"Then he must be a very stupid man."

"No, he isn't stupid," put in Uncle Philip mildly. "From what I've seen of him, I'd say he had a pretty good headpiece. After all, he's only doing what a lot of other men would do if they had the courage; he's refusing to accept defeat."

"That can be stupid," said my mother. She was rising and Uncle Philip was putting her fur over her shoulders. "Is he going to be at your party tomorrow?"

"Yes," I said.

The party was not exactly a success. Chess and Marya and I had at first invited only our parents; then panic set in and we felt that there must be other people present to prevent any possibility of difficult family discussions. I asked Uncle Philip and Chess asked a few of her friends and Marya invited everybody she could think of, and before we knew where we were, we had a real reception on our hands. Uncle Philip and Mr. Annuzio between them provided the drinks; my mother sent flowers and Joe and Basil came in after the shop closed and acted as waiters—but Marya's friends didn't mix well, and the company broke into two camps: the foreign side screeched loudly, and the English side endeavoured to make polite conversation above the din. Everybody was glad when it was over.

My mother was one of the first to leave, and Uncle Philip accompanied her. I saw them to the front door and my mother offered me her cheek, and thanked me.

"Can you come round tomorrow to see my new flat?" she asked.

"I'm sorry; not tomorrow," I said. "Tomorrow's Friday, and Marya and Chess and I are going to spend the week-end with Chess's parents. The three of us are meeting at the station after work, and going down together."

My mother frowned.

"But didn't I hear you telling somebody that you might have the afternoon off? You could come and have tea with me."

"If I get the afternoon off, I'll come," I said. " But it isn't certain that I will; the man I work for is going away and there'll be very little ... in fact, there'll be nothing for me to do, but unless he says I can go, I shan't be able to."

"Will you ring me up tomorrow and let me know?" she

asked.

I said that I would, and then they went away and I went back, reluctantly, to the drawing room.

I did get the afternoon off. I went home at midday and bought some food on the way from a delicatessen shop near the office. From the top of the bus as it went round Sloane Square, I caught sight of the car belonging to the South American couple who lived in the flat below ours; he was driving and she was sitting beside him. Their suitcases were at the back of the car, and I remembered that they, too, were going away for the week-end.

When I got home, I took my lunch out of the packages and ate it in the kitchen. I knew that I ought to ring up my mother and tell her that I would go round to see her, but I was enjoying my free afternoon, and decided that I would telephone later. First, I would wash my hair and put it into pins and read a book while it dried.

When I'd finished pinning up my hair, I telephoned to my mother and said that I would go and have tea with her on my way to the station to meet Chess and Marya. Then I took a book and heaped some cushions on the bedroom floor and put on the gas fire and lay with my head close to it to dry my hair. I had practically nothing on, and I was enjoying the feeling of freedom and leisure so much that I didn't even bother to do more than open the book; I just lay quietly, warm and at ease.

Then I lay even more quietly, for I heard a step on the landing. A moment afterwards, there was a token knock on the kitchen door and I recognised Mr. Flower's nervous cough. I wondered why he had come upstairs, and then remembered that he had promised to change the washer of one of the kitchen taps; if I kept quiet, it was not likely that he would walk along the corridor and look into our bedroom. Mrs. Flower would have done; in fact, we knew that she frequently did—but Mr. Flower had none of her impertinent curiosity.

I put my foot out and edged the door almost shut; then I leaned over and lowered the gas fire to lessen its hissing. I began to read, confident that he would not realise that I was in the flat; none of us, since Marya had begun to work, had ever been in on a week-day, and he would imagine himself alone.

I could hear him working, whistling softly and tunelessly as he always did when he was absorbed in a job. I could have spoken to him, but it seemed pointless. If he came into the corridor, I would call to him and tell him he couldn't come any further.

He finished the job and I heard him dropping his tools into the tool box—the little green one we had so often seen. Then I heard something else: the pring- pring-pring of the bell that was fixed to the back door of the Flowers' flat. It was a bicycle bell, put there by Mr. Flower; we could hear it from our bedroom, which had a window opening on to the little bleak back yard. We didn't often hear the bell, for as far as I knew, only the coalman rang it to get his money when he had emptied the bags of coal down the chute.

The bell rang again, and this time I knew Mr. Flower had

heard it, for he gave a sound like a soft grunt and then seemed to hesitate. Then he did what I knew he would do: he went into our bathroom and opened the window, which, like the bedroom window, looked down into the yard.

"Oh!" It was another grunt, this time unmistakably one of surprise. "Lookin' for me, Alice?" he called in his flat, unemphatic voice.

I didn't hear the reply, but there must have been one, for in a moment, Mr. Flower spoke again.

"Nope. Nobody in the 'ouse," he said. "I'm fixin' a washer on one o' the taps up 'ere . . . O.K. I'll be down."

He shut the bathroom window and went back to the kitchen. A moment later, I heard him go out on to the landing and lock the door behind him.

I relaxed; he was gone. I lay with the book on my stomach, too drowsy to find the page I had lost. My eyes began to close, and I hovered for a few moments between sleeping and waking, weaving an improbable romance around Mr. Flower and the unknown Alice. I wondered who she was. Mrs. Flower's name, I knew, wasn't Alice; it was Elsie.

I had an impulse—faint, fleeting—to get up and look down and glance at Alice. But I didn't get up.

Sometimes I look back and wonder what would have happened ... or if anything would have happened . . . if I had gone to the window. But I didn't go. I didn't want to be seen with my hair in pins, for one thing; for another, I was sleepy . . .

sleepier . . .

I fell into a doze. When I woke up, I saw that it was almost half past three; the gas fire had made the room too hot and my hair too dry. I dressed quickly, packed a small week-end case and then went downstairs and out of the house, on my way to my mother's new flat.

The place was, in its way, most impressive. I hadn't seen anything at all like it while I was looking for a flat, since the agent had shown me only those he considered within my price bracket. This one had everything: a luxury bathroom to each of the four luxury bedrooms and a double reception room in which you could, in which my mother probably would, entertain Royalty. There were press-button gadgets, and a bar that came out and a desk that disappeared, and a picture that swung out from the wall to reveal a hatch through to the kitchen; there was a maid's room fitted with a trim Swedish maid. As I said, most impressive. My mother showed me round without comment, but I knew that this was Mr. Annuzio's own method of providing a sharp contrast in modes of living.

The only contrast that made itself felt as far as I was concerned was that which existed between my mother's needs and mine; she was clearly delighted with it all, while I thought that it was about as homey as an executive suite. But I was delighted that she was delighted. Her liking for luxury always surprised me; she had a sort of greed for it that was, I would have said, unusual in somebody who had had so high a degree of comfort all her life. I would have liked to ask Uncle Philip to explain why his taste was so good and hers so appalling—but I knew that it was something I would have to work out for myself.

She gave me tea, and I drank it with one eye on the clock; then I thanked her and she kissed my cheek and I was off, with my suitcase, to meet Chess and Marya.

Chess was late. Marya was even later. I got into the train and tried to keep seats for them both, but it was quite hopeless, for the train was almost full when I arrived, and crammed to suffocation when at last Chess appeared. She was one of the last to get through the barrier, and Marya was positively the last and wouldn't have got through at all if it hadn't been for the fact that the ticket collector, on seeing her, couldn't find the strength to close the gate.

By that time, I'd lost both their seats and my own, so we stood all the way to Bridesbury, where we had to get out and change trains.

The second journey was short; not more than fifteen minutes, at the end of which we arrived at a small, cheerless station called Harly. There Chess's father awaited us, seated in an ancient and unsafe-looking vehicle which he called a trap. It had a small, raised seat behind, and on to this, as Chess and Marya and I took our places behind the Earl, scrambled a bent and withered old groom.

The Earl looked round at us and nodded genially by way of greeting. He was about seventy, with thick white hair and shaggy eyebrows and a craggy face. He was a mild man, but he had a startlingly harsh voice and manner.

We settled ourselves and he flicked the reins and shouted Giddon there to the pony. The pony, beyond turning its head to give us a contemptuous look, did not stir, so the Earl repeated the order with unprintable embellishments. The pony, probably shocked by the profanity, leapt forward, and the trap shot through the station entrance and out on to the narrow country road. The suddenness of the move sent the groom slithering dangerously to and fro on his little seat, and Chess and I clutched him just in time to save him from falling off the trap.

We had the road to ourselves, which was fortunate, as there was every few yards a corner which the Earl took at high speed, and on the wrong side. The road forked; the pony seemed to be taking the road on the right, but with shattering suddenness decided to go left. The trap rocked, Chess and Marya and I hung on desperately to our seats, but the groom had very little to hold on to. I saw him slipping and made a grab for him, but I was too late; he fell off, together with some parcels he had been holding, and rolled over in the roadway and then sat up watching us disappear into the distance.

Chess reported this loss to her father. As he did not seem to hear, she tapped him on the shoulder.

"Eh?" He half turned to look at her. "Say something?"

"Yes. Cookson. He fell off."

"Eh?"

"The groom. Cookson. He's fallen off."

"What—again?" ejaculated the Earl in disgust. "Damn feller's always doing it. When did he go?"

"Just now. Round that last corner. If you stop and turn—"

"Can't stop and can't turn," said the Earl. "Bally pony's got a mouth like iron. Can't get him moving on the way out and can't stop him on the way home. The basket go too?"

"If you mean the one Cookson was carrying—yes," said Chess.

"Then there goes the dinner," said the Earl. "Your mother won't like it." He jerked his head towards the orchards on either side of the road. "Looking lovely last week; gone off a bit now. Hold on."

The warning came only just in time for Marya and myself; Chess, more familiar with the local geography, was already gripping the rail of her seat. We had reached a rise in the road and I could see nothing, but the pony had swung to the right, and the trap missed by millimetres one side of a pair of heavy wrought-iron gates.

When I recovered my balance, I saw that we were driving along a thickly wooded avenue; over our heads the trees met, turning the road into a tunnel. The pony, glad to be home, broke into a gallop; the road rose steeply and then we had come to the end of the tunnel and were out in the daylight and I had my first view of Castle Harly, for three hundred years the seat of the Earls of Callerby.

I looked at it.

Take several hundred acres of bleak headland at the south-eastern tip of England. Erect a large Castle, so placed as to catch every wind that blows down the North Sea or up from the Channel. Build the south rooms at the foot of high cliffs and make the principal rooms face north. Decorate with battlements, and top with towers. Paint a backcloth of cold, grey, tossing sea.

Chess was watching my face.

"Well, here we are," said her father. "Francesca, take the pony's head." He got down from the creaking trap and held out a horny hand to assist us, but Marya and I were already out. "Let's get inside," he said. "Hope you don't expect to be comfortable; place hasn't been lived in—not to speak of—for a couple of hundred years."

The wind, which had become stronger and colder as we climbed the last half mile of the drive, blew our hair about our faces and whipped up our skirts. The Earl turned to lead us indoors, and Marya and I followed him while Chess drove the trap round to the stables.

The Earl pushed open a heavy oak door and we found ourselves in an enormous, bare hall of deadly coldness. We crossed it and walked down endless marble corridors; the only sounds were the Earl's heavy breathing and the click-click of Marya's four-inch heels on the marble.

"Bit bleak," said the Earl after a time. "Only about eight rooms got anything in 'em. Too cold to use the big rooms; we use the small ones round the kitchen."

Marya and I said nothing. She had a dazed look; perhaps she was thinking of a warm, crowded, colourful *hacienda.*

The Earl was throwing open the door of a room in which, at last, there was furniture. It was not a large room; it opened on to a small courtyard and had obviously been one of the meaner rooms of the Castle, but now it was carpeted and the windows were curtained. From a low sofa, Chess's mother rose to greet us.

"My dears, how nice to see you both! Come and warm yourselves."

We drew near to a vast fireplace in which stood a very small paraffin stove.

"It looks rather horrid, doesn't it?" said the Countess. "But while we're here, which fortunately is never for long, we're not concerned with looks; only with comfort and warmth. How is your mother, Denise? "

I said that my mother was in excellent health.

"Marya, does your father like his new house?"

Marya said that he liked it very much, and omitted to mention that a charming Italian lady was sharing it with him. Then Chess came in and her mother kissed her and enquired about the shopping that the Earl had been commissioned to do before meeting us at the station, and learned that it was with the groom, somewhere between the Castle and the village.

"Oh, dear, oh, dear!" The Countess's voice lifted and fell. She was large and bosomy and had a deceptively motherly look. “Well, we must just make the best of it, that’s all. We’ll manage something.”

I learned, before the week-end was over, that when the Countess said ‘we’ in connection with any work that was to be done, she didn’t mean we; she meant you-all.

Chess was ushering Marya and myself out of the drawing room and up to our bedroom. We found ourselves embarking on an even longer and colder walk than the one we had just taken with the Earl. This time we were carrying our suitcases, which Chess had put into the hall.

We negotiated the grand staircase and were led by Chess to a humbler stone one.

“But I do not understand,” protested Marya, panting. “Your father said that you live only in the rooms close to the kitchen.”

“He and my mother do, but I’ve got a room up here. You’ll see why I like it.”

She opened a door, and we saw.

We were in a massive chamber which, like our drawing room at the flat, had windows that faced two ways. But there the resemblance ended. These windows were set in walls ten feet thick, and when Marya and I walked up to them and looked out at the view, neither of us could utter any adequate comment.

“Gosh!” I said at last.

It was a poor tribute to the magnificent seascape that

stretched below and beyond the windows. The Castle seemed to have risen directly from the sea; waves tumbled against the walls, hissed and fell back upon oncoming waves. Ships, large and small, rode the rough sea; gulls wheeled on a level with our heads, turned to regard us with one suspicious eye and then swooped away. It was a breath-taking prospect—but it was not a warm or a friendly one. It was remote, and a little sinister, and terribly lonely.

"There's a bathroom about a quarter of a mile down the corridor when you want one," said Chess. " No h, and not much c, but we'll bring some hot water with us when we come upstairs to bed. I put you both in here with me because I thought—"

"You thought right," I said. "In a place like this, what you crave is company. Do we all sleep in that four-poster?"

"There's room and to spare," said Chess. "Let's go down; we've got to get the dinner."

Marya looked at her.

"But is there nobody to help your father and your mother?"

"The groom fell off—remember?" said Chess. "So did the butler, cook and handyman."

We paused to contemplate this multiple loss.

"Some old women come in from the village in relays," said Chess. "Let's go down. If my father offers you sherry, say no."

"Why?" demanded Marya. "I need to drink."

"Just say no," said Chess, leading us downstairs. "It's a special brand he keeps for people he thinks, nearly always rightly, aren't worth giving drinks to because he's sure that half the time they've no idea what they're drinking."

Before we had sorted out this involved sentence, we had arrived at the kitchen. Entering, we saw that it was in almost every respect what it had been three hundred years before—but in one corner stood a coke-burning stove, over which an old woman bent, peering into saucepans. She looked up as we came in, and gave a toothless smile.

"Good evening," said Chess.

"Good evenin', m'lady. Got it all going nicely, I have. But Cookson didn't come in."

"He fell off the trap," explained Chess.

"Wouldn't you think he'd learn?" exclaimed the crony. "Well, I've got the joint in the oven, m'lady, and I'll stay and wash up if you'd like me to."

Chess thanked her, and then we joined the Earl and Countess. We were given no choice as to whether we would or wouldn't drink sherry, as the Earl, after a suspiciously short search, announced that he must have finished the last bottle and forgotten to order any more.

I was hungry, and so were Chess and Marya; the thought of the joint sustained us. But when it was brought to the dinner table and the Earl began to carve, it became clear that it was intended not only for dinner, but also for the week-end. The three of us filled up on bread and butter and cheese.

We would have liked to have gone to bed soon after dinner, but only Chess and Marya got away; I was cornered, as I knew I would be, by the Countess.

She went, to my relief, straight to the point.

"You know, Denise, don't you, that Francesca's father and I are very worried about the extraordinary way in which she's behaving over her engagement?"

I said that I had some idea.

"We spoke to Stephen; he feels, naturally, that Francesca should make the first move. We spoke to her, but she persists in declaring that she is in love with this man Edward. We made some enquiries about him when we were in Bermuda; we learned nothing to his discredit, thank goodness, but he cannot be compared with Stephen."

Financially he couldn't, I thought—but did not say.

"I do feel—don't you, Denise?—that Francesca owes us some consideration. We have come all the way to England to try to help her; we came away just when it seemed that somebody was going to offer us a cottage, and we do feel that Francesca should come and spend some time with us here, and then we could ask Stephen down and we could all talk things over sensibly. If she goes on as she's doing, I'm afraid she'll antagonise Stephen altogether, and we feel that would be a great pity. One doesn't want to appear mercenary, but he has so much to give her; he could make her so happy. To throw herself away ... it would be such a *tragedy,* Denise. We have had such hopes for her . . . such hopes. Her father and I have always done our best for her, and now ...”

I looked hard at her, and saw that she actually meant it. It was fantastic. Whenever Chess had needed her parents, they had been playing bridge on the fringes of the Mediterranean or the Caribbean. But the Countess, sitting beside me on the sofa, had the air of a mother whose life had been one long sacrifice for her daughter and who now saw the years of effort wasted.

The large face turned to mine. As well as looking motherly, she looked sensible; whoever it was who said that looks are deceivers, knew what he was talking about.

“You must do something, Denise,” she urged. “You must use your influence. Nobody can do more with Francesca than you; you must speak to her. You must make her see that she is throwing herself away.”

I felt sorry for her. What Chess was throwing away was benefits for the family. Stephen, rich, open- handed, was slipping away. The gleam of gold was proving a mirage.

The next day, the Earl was franker. Having got me alone, he stated his case in one brief sentence.

“Would have been nice,” he said, “to have had some money in the family at last.”

It was during the afternoon. I had climbed along a rocky path to a point at which I could get an uninterrupted view of the sea. Chess and her mother, with Marya, were some distance below me, picking cherries from a few neglected trees. The Earl came slowly up the path to join me, and I made room for him on the slab of rock on which I was sitting. After his opening sentence, he sat looking broodingly at the Castle.

"Never could make up my mind," he said slowly, "whether the damn place's ugliness was its undoing. I mean to say, if it hadn't been so hideous, perhaps one or two of my ancestors might have tried to make something of it. But none of 'em ever did; from first to last, they made a point of gettin' out and staying out. Can't blame 'em; did the same myself. The trouble was always the same: lack of money. They created the first Earl in 1760 and they lopped his head off in 1766, and with his head went all his estates—except this one. They'd have confiscated this too, I dare say, if they could've found any takers."

"After you—" I said, and paused.

"After me, it all goes. The heir's an American citizen, and he's not interested. He came over here a few years ago to have a look round; I came to England to meet him and I brought him down here, but we chose a bad week-end. There's always a strong wind, but when we arrived, there was a howling gale and he bally near took off over the cliffs. I put him in a vault of a bedroom and told him it was haunted, but even that didn't tempt him; he drove away next morning and I haven't heard from him since." He sighed. " Oh, well, no use worrying. No use trying to talk to Francesca, either. At her age . . . your age, money doesn't seem to matter. She'll throw away this Stephen and his millions without a thought—but as I said, we could have used some of his money. Think she'll marry that other feller?"

I said that at this stage, it was impossible to say.

"Would have been nice to have been able to warm up this place a bit," said the Earl. "As well as that, we could have bought a little place in London, or a nice little property in one of the sterling areas. We could have . . . Oh, well, as I said; no use brooding. Francesca'll marry whoever she wants to, I dare say. If you could put in a word, I'd be grateful. You might be able to make her see it from our point of view."

That seemed to be the end of our talk. We rose and walked slowly down to join the others. As we drew near, the Earl's eyes rested on Marya.

"Handsome gal," he remarked. "Is it true she'll inherit several millions?"

I nodded, and he sighed once more.

"Pity Chess wasn't a boy," he said.

Chess and Marya and I caught an early train home on Sunday evening. We shared a taxi from Victoria, but Chess and Marya dropped me at Uncle Philip's Club; he was to give me supper before going away again on a brief business trip.

When supper was over, he put me into a taxi and paid the driver and I was driven to Stacey Square. I let myself into the house, noting with some surprise that every curtain in the Flowers' flat was closely drawn.

This was unusual, for they never drew the curtains of their bedroom before retiring for the night; we had got into the habit of looking to see if the window was screened, and lowering our voices if it was. Tonight, they seemed to have gone to bed very early indeed.

I went up the stairs, and on the first landing found myself colliding with the South American, who was on his way from the middle-floor kitchen to the drawing room.

"Did you enjoy your week-end?" I asked.

To my amazement, he made no reply. He seemed about to speak, and then stopped.

"You have not heard?" he said at last.

"Heard what?" I asked.

"About the ... the accident?"

"Accident!" My face must have gone white, for his wife, who had come to their drawing room door, hurried forward and took me by the arm.

"Do not worry," she said. "It is not Chess, or Marya."

"Then—?"

Husband and wife exchanged glances and he said something to her in rapid Spanish. Then he looked at me.

"Go upstairs," he said. "They will tell you."

I took the last flight of stairs at a run, and opened our drawing room door. There were three people in the room: Chess and Marya—and Fergus Maitland. They turned as I came in.

"What's happened?" I asked.

There was a pause. They seemed to be waiting for one another to speak. It was Fergus who told me the news at last.

"Your landlord, Mr. Flower ... is dead," he said quietly.

I stared at him, and something seemed to ring in my head. A bell. A bicycle bell . . .

"When . . . how did it happen?" I brought out.

"They found him on Friday evening at about half past four," said Fergus, "in the kitchen of his own flat."

"Found him ...?"

"With a knife in his back," said Fergus.

Chapter Five

I don't know what I looked like when I had grasped the significance of what Fergus had said.

I don't even know how long it was that he stood there, or how long the others waited for my reaction. I was staring at a mental picture of myself lying on the floor of the bedroom, keeping very quiet so that Mr. Flower would not know that I was there. Mr. Flower . . .

"Don't take it like that, Denny," I heard Chess saying gently. "Maybe he's ... I mean, he couldn't have been too happy, could he, pushed around by his wife . . ."

Her words of consolation trailed away. Life with Mrs. Flower was a better thing than a knife in the back.

"I didn't know you liked him so much," Marya said, watching my face.

"I . . . When did you hear?" I asked them.

"Fergus was here in the flat, waiting for us," said Marya. "Mrs. Flower let him have a key, because he wanted to be here when we came home; he wanted to tell us the news quietly, instead of letting other people tell us."

"It was in the papers on Saturday," Fergus said. "I felt pretty sure that none of you would see it; that is, I didn't think you'd be reading the kind of paper that made it front page news. I saw it on a poster when I was out on Saturday morning, and I bought a paper and read about it. It didn't say much: Mrs. Flower had been expecting him at the coffee bar, and he didn't turn up. She sent someone round; the kitchen door wasn't locked, and . . ."

Chess and Marya, I learned, on coming home earlier, had noticed nothing unusual about the house—except a policeman who seemed to be strolling aimlessly to and fro. But ten minutes after their arrival, a police officer had called and questioned them.

"All he wanted to know," Chess said, "is where we all were on Friday afternoon. I told him. I said we'd all been at work until about five; then we'd all met at the station and gone down to stay with my mother and father. The Inspector, or whoever he was, thanked us and said he wouldn't bother us again; he'd talked to the people in the middle flat and found they'd left the house early on Friday afternoon and gone down to the country."

"Yes, I—"

I stopped. I had begun to say that I had seen them from the top of the bus—and then I remembered. Remembered that once I revealed that fact, I would be revealing everything: my free afternoon, which I had forgotten to mention to Chess and Marya; my presence in the flat. Even if I said nothing of Mr.

Flower's having been there too, it was more than likely that his wife, who had always made a point of knowing where he was and what he was doing, would remember that he had said something about fixing a washer. They would find, if they looked, a new washer on the tap in the kitchen.

I felt sick. I saw the eyes of the others on me, and made a strong effort to speak naturally.

"Is Mrs. Flower in the house?" I asked.

"No. Her sister came and took her away for a few days," said Fergus.

A sister . . . Alice . . .

"Mrs. Flower collapsed on Friday evening," went on Fergus, "and the police got hold of her sister— she was on holiday in Guernsey, and she flew over. She's apparently the only close relation. She waited until Mrs. Flower felt well enough to travel, and they went away last night."

In Guernsey . . . then she couldn't have been Alice.

"If I'd known you were going to be so upset," said Chess, looking at me with a worried frown, "I'd have saved the news till the morning."

"Did you like poor little Mr. Flower so much?" asked Marya.

"You don't have to like somebody to feel sick when you hear he's been murdered," I said. "Will the . . ."

"Will the what?" asked Chess.

"Will the police keep a watch on the house from now on?"

"They may," said Fergus, "but I doubt it. If they do, they'll do it discreetly. They won't bother any of you. There was a small crowd of sightseers on Saturday, and a few people this morning, but they'd gone by this afternoon. The local interest has, I think, died."

Died. Mr. Flower had died. Somebody—Alice—had called to him at about . . . what time was it? I had got home at about one fifteen; I'd eaten my lunch by about two or two fifteen; hair wash, hair set; that would take about three quarters of an hour, so that by about three o'clock I was lying on the bedroom floor drying my hair. I hadn't looked at the clock until I woke up from the doze I'd fallen into; it was then half past three. So between three and half past—

I looked at Fergus.

"What time do they think he was ..."

"Murdered?" Fergus spoke quietly. "He was found at half past four. They think he'd been dead for about an hour."

So he had gone down, and Alice had been there. But perhaps Alice hadn't been alone. Women named Alice, I felt vaguely, were quiet women; good women; the Alices didn't drive knives into men's backs. Not gentle, harmless men like Mr. Flower.

"I think," I heard Fergus saying, "it would be a good idea if we all had a drink."

There wasn't much, but what there was we drank, and I felt a little better. Fergus, empty glass in hand, looked at us and spoke in his usual unhurried way.

"I suggest a small dinner out tomorrow evening," he said. "This is an ugly thing to have to come home to. If I might offer myself . . ."

Chess couldn't; she was going out with Edward. Marya was dining with Laurie.

"You go, Denny," urged Marya. "It will do you good. You cannot stay here in the flat alone so soon after the . . . the accident, thinking and thinking. Make her go, Chess."

"I should be very happy to take you," said Fergus.

"Thank you. I . . . It's very kind of you," I said. "I'd like to go."

He bowed. Then he carried the empty glasses into the kitchen, washed them and went away.

We were sorry, for the first time, to see him go, and we felt grateful to have had him with us while we absorbed the shock of the news. Left alone, we found ourselves going round doing something we had never thought of doing before: locking the drawing room windows before going to bed.

I wanted to be alone; to be quiet; to clear, if I could, some of the confusion from my brain. I wanted to work out how much, if any, responsibility I had in the matter; I wanted to reconstruct every detail of Friday afternoon. But Chess and Marya were watching me. At first they made no comment upon my long and brooding silences, but when I had let the basin in the bathroom overflow, Chess came in and turned off the taps, and Marya mopped up the water on the floor; then they led me into the bedroom and made me sit on my bed.

"Now," said Chess, seating herself with Marya on her own bed. "Something's the matter. What is it?"

"To be upset about poor Mr. Flower, that is natural," said Marya. "But to worry too much is not good. He is dead and you can do nothing."

Before I could stop myself, I had spoken my thoughts aloud.

"I could have looked out of the window," I said.

There was a pause.

"Looked out of what window, and when?" asked Chess slowly at last.

"I was in the flat," I said. "And he was here too."

The pause this time was longer. Looking across at the two of them, I saw the colour draining slowly out of their cheeks, and I was sorry that I had spoken. But to speak of it was already giving me relief. Now that I had begun, I wanted to go on.

"You mean that Mr. Flower—" began Marya.

"—was up here," I said. " I had Friday afternoon off. I came home and had lunch here and then I washed my hair and did what we always do—I lay on the floor in here, drying it by the gas fire. And Mr. Flower came upstairs to fix the washer on the kitchen tap, and I heard him, but I said nothing because I looked so awful with my hair in curlers—and I didn't have much on."

I stopped to draw a deep breath—the first draught of air I seemed to have taken since I came home and heard the news.

"Go on," said Chess. "The window."

"Well, someone rang the back door bell and—"

"The bicycle bell fixed to their back door?" Marya stopped me to ask.

"Yes. I heard it, but I don't think he did, the first time. It rang again and he went into the bathroom and opened the window to see who it was. Then he made a sound—as though he'd recognised whoever it was but wasn't too pleased to see them; a kind of ' Oh, it's you, is it? ' sound."

"And then?" Chess asked.

"Then he closed the window and went downstairs. He collected his tools first."

I came to a halt, and the other two looked at me. Chess was frowning; Marya was looking bewildered.

"What time was this?" asked Chess.

"As near as I can make out, about three."

"Three. So he went down, and by half past three they think he was dead. It's a pity," said Chess slowly, "that you didn't look out of that window."

"I think that it is good that she did not," said Marya. "If she had seen him, he—"

"She," I said.

Chess stared at me.

"I thought you said you didn't look out of the window."

"I didn't. But it was someone called Alice. I heard the name."

"Alice?" repeated Marya. "You are sure?"

"I'm quite sure. After all, the bathroom's only about five yards away, and this door was slightly open."

"What exactly did Mr. Flower say?" asked Chess.

"He said, I think: ' Looking for me, Alice?' "

"And then he went downstairs and ..." Marya shivered.

"It couldn't have happened like that," said Chess after a few moments, her tone positive. "It couldn't. Do you mean to tell me that a woman would walk up and ring a back door bell, call someone down and plunge a knife into his back? That's crazy! Why, just imagine! She would have been seen coming and going."

"Would she?" I asked.

They both knew what I meant. The back door of the Flowers' flat could be reached in two ways: from Stacey Street, or by a long, narrow passage that ran behind a high wall backing the houses on Stacey Street, and came out into the courtyard of a converted mews behind the King's Road. If anyone wanted to come unseen to the Flowers' back door, it would be easy for them to glance along the length of the passage, make certain that it was clear, and dart swiftly up it. Damp and dark, it was seldom used except by school children scurrying by a short cut to school, or very occasionally by women with their hair in curlers, slipper-clad, hoping to be unobserved as they hurried out for a forgotten item of shopping. It would not be difficult to come and to go unseen.

There was in all our minds, I knew, a picture of Stacey Street and a memory of the varied types of women we saw at the doors of the mean little houses. Some of the women were clean and respectable; others were slatterns. From the latter group, we could without difficulty have picked more than one harridan capable of swooping on the meek little Mr. Flower . . .

"Perhaps," said Chess suddenly, "he wasn't like that at all."

"Like what?" asked Marya.

"Meek, kind, gentle. He might have been one of those men who led a double life. He might have—"

"If he was," I said, "Mrs. Flower must have been leading it too, because the only time he was out of her sight was when he was cleaning up the flats or working in them. She saw him in the mornings and she saw him every evening and if she wanted him in between times, all she had to do was step round the corner from the coffee bar. I don't see how a man could lead a double life in circumstances like those."

"But . . . but why would anyone kill him?" asked Chess in a puzzled voice. "What I mean is, what would they kill him or? Nothing had been stolen; nothing had been touched, the police said."

"He was not rich," said Marya. "It would not have been for money."

"I don't suppose there was any money in the house anyhow," said Chess. "We pay the rent by cheque, and I know that Mr. Flower's last job when the coffee bar shut every evening was to trot out with the takings and put them into the night safe of the Bank."

"But if not money, what then?" went on Marya. "Not love. Who could love poor little Mr. Flower?"

We sat in silence and wondered. Who indeed? Plain little, timid little, browbeaten little Mr. Flower.

"Even if somebody had loved him, which I hope they did," said Chess after a time, "I can't believe that anybody would have felt so strongly about him that they'd be driven to plunging a knife in his back. He doesn't go with thwarted passion, somehow."

We had to agree that he didn't. But whether from motives of piracy or passion, someone had come to the house and stabbed Mr. Flower and left him dead in his dreary little kitchen.

I broke a silence that had lasted for some minutes.

"I suppose I'll have to tell them," I said.

The other two looked at me uncomprehendingly.

"Tell who what?" enquired Chess.

"I suppose I'll have to tell the police." I saw that neither of them had understood the import of what I had said, and reframed the sentence. "I'll have to go and tell the police that I was in the flat that afternoon and—"

Marya's gasp of horror stopped me.

"Tell them?" she brought out with difficulty. "Tell the *police?"*

"You must be out of your mind," said Chess.

I looked from one to the other.

"You don't understand," I said patiently. "Mr. Flower was murdered. Just before he was murdered, I was here, and I heard him—"

"You're crazy," broke in Chess. "Do you mean to say that just because we're sitting here trying to find a connection between a woman called Alice and the murder, there must necessarily have been? What could you tell the police, if you were so demented as to go to them? What would you say to them? Mr. Flower, you'd tell them, looked out of the window and said he'd go downstairs. And he went down. And then? He could have seen Alice and settled any business she'd wanted to settle; there was time enough for that. How do you know that there wasn't someone hiding in the kitchen, waiting for her to go away? When Alice had gone, they could have come out and killed Mr. Flower. So what happens if you rush to the nearest police station and tell your story? You involve this Alice, who might have had not the smallest connection with the affair. What's more—"

"What is more," said Marya, "it will be the end of us in

this flat."

"I don't understand," I said.

"It will be the end," she said, her hands coming into play to accentuate her words. "You go to the police; so. At once you are mixed up in this thing. The police will come, they will look at this bedroom, at the bathroom window; you will have to say to them: 'I was lying here in this room, and Mr. Flower was in the kitchen.' They will ask you about time: 'What time, exactly; try to think,' they will say to you. The newspapers will say about you, that you were here. And then? My father, Chess's father—what will they do? Do you think that they will not be filled with horror that we are mixed up with this? Do you think—"

"But I *know* something," I said. "I have to tell the police what I know."

"If you do, something much more serious than horrified parents will come out of it," said Chess slowly. "Think, Denny: there's been a murder, and the police don't know who did it. Whoever did it might be living close to us. Whoever did it will hear that you went to the police, and will wonder exactly how much you know. Whoever did it will panic . . . and then?"

"Then," said Marya, "we shall all be murdered, all three of us. The murderer will say to himself . . . herself: ' What one girl knows, she will have told the other two girls.' " She shuddered. "Denny, you are making me frightened."

"There's a right and a wrong in this," I insisted. "If you're a good citizen, you line yourself up on the side of the police.

If you know something that can help them to find a criminal, you—"

"Yes; if you really *know* something," said Chess. "If you have some definite, concrete information to give, it's your duty as a citizen to give it. If you hear a scream, and you look out and see a man hurrying away, or a woman; a man or woman you can identify, pick out of an identity parade . . . that's information. If during our life in the flat, we'd ever seen or heard of a woman called Alice . . . that's information. But all you can give the police is a scrap of coincidence: you were in this flat on the afternoon of the murder and a woman called Alice spoke to Mr. Flower. What help will that be? What help would it possibly be—to the police or to poor Mr. Flower? He's dead. The police will look into his history and find out if anybody had a motive for killing him—and they'll work from there. You can't go to them and incriminate some probably perfectly blameless woman called Alice."

"If she's perfectly blameless, she'll be able to prove it," I said.

"And would you like that somebody should point a finger at you and say to the police: 'Perhaps she did the murder.' Would you?" demanded Marya.

"I don't suppose I would," I said. "But I can't just go on with my life, calmly forgetting about Friday afternoon and Mr. Flower and Alice, can I?"

"If you're wise, you will," said Chess. "You've got no real information to give—at least, in my opinion you haven't. How many Alices are there in London? Do the police have to round them up and interview them all?"

"You must forget about it," said Marya.

"We must all forget about it," said Chess. "We've got to put the whole thing out of our minds—and not utter a single word about this to any living soul."

"That is wise," said Marya.

That seemed to be the last word; we settled ourselves in our several beds and the lights were put out and there was nothing to do but sleep.

But I couldn't sleep. I lay awake and heard the hours of the night striking: one, two, three. Four . . .

My mind was in confusion, but of one thing I was certain: I could not resume my normal way of life and brush aside the events of Friday afternoon. I did not know who should be told, or what value my information might have; all I knew was that I should make the facts available to the authorities. I didn't want to involve an innocent woman—but she, like myself, might have been caught in the net of tragedy; like me, she could prove that she was not criminally involved.

I turned the matter over and over—and then, with the first rays of dawn came the solution of the problem.

I would tell Uncle Philip. I had been a fool not to think of him before. He was away in Brussels on business, but only for three days. He would return, and I would tell him what I knew—and he would tell me what to do.

There was nothing to worry about. Everything would be all right. Uncle Philip would handle the whole thing.

So believing, I fell asleep.

Chapter Six

On the following evening, Fergus Maitland arrived at the flat just after Edward, who had arrived just after Laurie. We all went out of the house together, and parked between Edward's and Laurie's cars I saw a very large, very old vehicle that seemed to be held together by straps. The hood was down, and on the back seat rested a picnic hamper. On this, Edward's eyes rested.

"Bit large for two, isn't it?" he asked. "What have you got in it?"

"Cold chicken and some rather special cheese," Fergus told him, "and a cold meat pie and some sausage rolls and—"

"Who're you feeding?" asked Chess in a surprised tone. "The Boys' Brigade?"

Edward had lifted the lid of the hamper and was peering inside.

"Looks good stuff," he said wistfully. He was very thin indeed and he looked as though more good stuff in his youth would have made better stuff of him. He glanced at Chess. "I suppose you wouldn't care to join up and—"

"No," said Chess.

"Oh, well." Edward, with an effort, closed the lid and turned his mind from food. He led Chess to his car, and they followed Laurie and Marya; Portholes and I were left. He handed me into his car and took his place by my side.

"Why is this car like Chess's father?" he asked, as he started the engine.

I had no idea.

"Because she's ancient but noble," he explained. "She must be all of forty-two; they say it's a skittish age, so perhaps that's why she's been giving a bit of trouble lately." He glanced at me. "Comfy?"

"Yes, thank you."

He relapsed into silence, looking at the road ahead; I looked at the shops and houses we were passing. The traffic thinned, the shops and houses became more widely separated, and soon we were nosing our way to the edge of a grassy slope beside the river. Fergus switched off the engine, got out a rug and laid it on the grass, and placed the hamper beside it.

"I should have asked you whether you wanted a picnic meal," he said, as we settled ourselves, "but when I saw how warm and sunny it was going to be, I knew you'd rather be out of doors. Half a minute; I'll get you a cushion."

It was quiet and pleasant and peaceful. He handed me food and wine, and we ate and drank. The cheese proved to be smoked; smoked cheese and Marya, explained Fergus, were his twin passions.

"Were you," he asked, between bites of a chicken leg, "very friendly with your late landlord?"

I looked at him in surprise.

"Mr. Flower? No. But . . . I liked him."

The pleasure of the picnic faded a little; I had almost forgotten the flat, and Mr. Flower. I wished Fergus had not brought up the subject, but he seemed determined to pursue it.

"Landlady back?" he enquired.

"No. At least, I don't think so. Their flat . . . her flat still seems shut up."

"Any theories?" he asked.

I felt my colour rising; it was difficult not to remember last night, when Chess and Marya and I had sat in the bedroom putting forward several improbable ones.

"None," I said.

"I just asked," said Fergus, "because the news seemed to hit you rather hard. Chess and Marya were shocked, but you . . ."

"Well?"

"You looked frightened," he said.

"Well, I wasn't," I told him. "At least," I amended, "murder is always frightening, and when it happens just two floors below you, that's too close."

"Much too close," he agreed. "More salad?"

"No, thank you; in fact, I can't eat one more thing."

He filled my glass from the almost empty wine bottle and then, without moving his body, stretched out an arm, collected the remains of the picnic item by item and put them back into the hamper and closed it.

"It was a wonderful meal," I said gratefully, "and it's nice to be out here."

"When does your uncle get back?" he asked.

"In three days."

"In time for your mother's house-warming party," he said.

"The day before." I looked at him and tried to conceal my surprise. "Did she—"

"—ask me? She was kind enough to do so," said Fergus with the kind of grave, mock formality I was getting used to. "Great big card with great big gold letters. I've got it up on my mantelpiece; very impressive."

"Are you going?"

"But yes!" His eyes opened wide behind his glasses. "You think I'd pass up a chance to get into the most récherché circle in London? No, Ma'am! All my favourite stars brushing by me, closer than they've ever brushed before; the lions and lionesses of the theatre all performing for my benefit—and without charge; and your beautiful mother holding my hand and saying 'How kind of yoooo to come.' Miss it? But no! I—" He paused to peer at me. "You don't mean to say you're not going?"

"Of course I'm going. So is Marya. So is Chess."

And their parents, and Stephen and Laurie and Edward. I knew they had all been asked, but I did not think that my mother would have extended the invitation to Portholes. I decided that it must be because she was having difficulty in finding enough presentable young men to even up the numbers at the party.

"You're not like your mother," said Fergus, studying me frankly.

"No. I'm said to be like my father."

There was a pause. Then:

"Where is he?" asked Fergus.

"My father? He's in Singapore."

"Doing what?"

"Doing business with his partners."

"No wife?"

"No."

"He remains faithful to the memory of your mother?"

"If I ever meet him, I'll ask him," I said.

He was watching me, and I had an odd feeling, not for the first time in our acquaintance, that he was talking on one subject and pondering on one totally different. When he had finished studying me, his gaze rested on the river, and I looked at him and saw things that I had not seen before: his long, bony hands; his stiff, unruly hair; his high cheek-bones and straight nose and strong-looking chin. Not handsome, I decided, but far and away more interesting looking than any of the men

Marya had chosen instead of him. Soon, I hoped, she would grow tired of Laurie and learn to appreciate Portholes.

And in the meantime, I was enjoying myself. He was a restful companion; he talked, when he talked, slowly and without emphasis; his silences were long and easy.

That was our first outing—but the next evening, I found myself out with him again. It was raining, and we did not picnic; we ate at a small riverside restaurant and sat on after dinner watching the boats going by.

"Where do you live?" I asked him, out of a long and companionable silence.

"Meryl Street."

"Where's that?"

"A stone's throw from Buckingham Palace. If I had the time, I'd pop in from time to time to see how they were all getting on in there. I've got a nice flat, if you'd ever care to look at it."

"How many rooms?"

"Four—and what the agents call the usual offices. The furniture's mine; I've got the place on a long lease. Speaking of leases," he asked, "how long did you three sign on for?"

"A year."

"You think you'll all last the course?"

"Why shouldn't we?"

"I gather that your several parents—"

"We haven't heard from them since the week-end."

"Which means that they haven't read about the murder. Or, having read that a man was murdered, haven't the remotest idea that it could have any connection with you."

"That's what we're hoping," I said, and found his frowning gaze coming to rest on me.

"You mean you're not going to tell them?" he asked incredulously.

"If we do, you know quite well what'll happen," I said. " Chess wouldn't be allowed to stay there for another day. Nor would Marya."

"And you don't feel that you ought to tell—"

"Yes, we ought to," I acknowledged.

"But you're not going to? "

"We're not going to. The only person I'm going to talk to," I said, "is my Uncle Philip."

"And if he wants to tell your mother?"

"He won't want to."

Fergus said nothing more. He drove me home and we went up to the flat; he helped himself to a drink out of the store he now kept there, and then took his leave.

The others were not in. I had a bath and went to bed and was not long in falling asleep. There was no longer any reason to lie awake worrying. Uncle Philip would be back tomorrow and I was going to see him and tell him everything.

I came out of oblivion some time later and reached sleepily for the alarm clock. Then I realised that it wasn't the bell of the alarm that had wakened me; it was the telephone.

I switched on the bedside light and looked at the time: three-thirty. I glanced at Chess; she was deep in sleep. I got out of bed and pattered to the telephone in the corridor, picked it up and heard Marya's voice.

She sounded cool and factual. She was at the Caribbean, she told me, and she was going on with Laurie Gale to his flat.

"I tell you this," she said, "because after what happened to . . . after what happened, you and Chess might be frightened if I did not come home and telephone to the . . . But there is no need to do that," she ended.

"But look here—" I began. Then I stopped; she had rung off.

I went back slowly to the bedroom and got into bed. It wasn't, I told myself firmly, my business. If Marya wanted to make Laurie Gale a present of another easy success, she was perfectly free to do so; I couldn't stop her. All I had to do was go back to bed and sleep.

I was settling myself when Chess stirred, and I saw her head come up sleepily.

"Hm?" she murmured interrogatively.

"Telephone," I said.

She shook the sleep from her eyes and glanced at the clock and then back at me.

"At this time of night?"

"Morning."

"Who?"

"Marya. To say she wasn't coming home."

Chess raised herself on one elbow.

"Where's she going? To her father's?"

"To Laurie Gale's. She rang up because she thought that after what happened to Mr. Flower, we might be in such a state of nerves that we'd panic and ring up the police."

There was a pause.

"Is she going in a party?" Chess was sitting upright, in bed, hugging her knees.

"It didn't sound like it."

There was a longer pause.

If she does," said Chess at last, "she's a bigger fool than I would ever have taken her for."

She was throwing back the bedclothes and reaching for her slippers, and I didn't have to ask where she was going. Problems, which removed most people's appetite, invariably made Chess ravenously hungry. I followed her into the kitchen and stood watching as she cut herself a large lump of cheese and bit into it. Neither of us spoke for some time.

"I don't believe she'd go to his flat and spend the rest of the night there," said Chess slowly at last.

"Then why should she ring up at this hour and go to the trouble of telling us that that was what she was doing?"

Chess finished the cheese and tore open a packet of wheaten biscuits. We pulled out chairs and sat down, our elbows on the little plastic-covered table, and for a time the only sound was that of Chess crunching.

"No," she said at last.

"No what?"

"South American or not," said Chess, "she's as cool as they come. And she knows this Gale's record. If she's changed her mind about hopping into bed with someone before being married to them—which I doubt—she wouldn't choose a professional charmer like Gale. You must have got that phone message wrong."

"I didn't get it wrong."

"Then she's up to something. I don't know what it is, but it isn't letting herself become one more notch on Laurie Gale's scoreboard."

"But—"

"I'll bet you this tin of beans," said Chess, opening it energetically, "that I'm right. She takes the longterm view, does Marya. She believes that it's easy to hop into bed but clever to stay out. Pass me a spoon out of that drawer, will you?"

I passed the spoon, and Chess ate the beans from the tin.

"And now let's get back to bed," she said, when she had finished them. "You had me worried for a moment, but you should know Marya by this time."

We went back to bed and put out the lights and I lay in the darkness wishing I had Chess's calm conviction that the telephone call had meant nothing in particular. Marya had once shared our views, but people change their views, and we hadn't had time, lately, to discuss abstract matters. When we had talked, it had been not of men but of money. Money, money, money. We had sat round the kitchen table working out not the present-day relations between men and women, but who owed whom how much, and for what. Our discussions were purely financial; we budgeted, we added up columns of figures and got a different total each time, and we wrote complicated shopping lists and decided who should bring home the bread and the fruit and the vegetables, and leave the grocery order at Preston's. We talked shopping as we dressed in the morning, and money if we met at night. We were shut up at work all day, and into the few remaining hours of the day we had to fit our private lives: cooking, cleaning, shoes to be taken to the menders, clothes to the cleaners, laundry to the launderette. There hadn't been much time to find out whether our views on men and marriage had changed.

I heard Chess's voice.

"Listen!" she said.

I listened. A taxi engine throbbing outside; the taxi door banging.

I got out of bed and pulled aside the curtain and looked down on to the back yard, beyond which we could sometimes see cars that had stopped on the corner. But I could see nothing. By the time I had turned away, we had heard the front door closing, and then Marya's key was turning in the door that led from the landing into the kitchen. She put on a light and glanced up the corridor and saw me standing in my far-from-glamorous pyjamas, staring at her. For a moment she stared back, and then she began to laugh helplessly, leaning against the kitchen door and shaking with uncontrollable mirth.

"For goodness' sake," Chess called to her, "let the poor girl get to bed. You had her worried."

Marya, still laughing, walked into our bedroom and sat on my bed.

"Don't settle down there," said Chess. "We want some sleep."

Marya's eyes were on me; she had stopped laughing.

"You do not mean to say that you were worried about me?" she asked.

"Why ring up and say you weren't coming home? Why give me the idea that you were spending the rest of the night—morning—with Laurie Gale?" I asked.

"But I had to say that," said Marya. "He was standing there when I was telephoning. I could not explain to you. But I thought that you would understand."

"Well, she didn't," said Chess, pulling the sheets round her chin. "But you did," she went on, "go to his flat?"

"I went, yes," said Marya. "I went because for two weeks without stopping, he has pestered me. For two weeks he said all the time, all the time, that we must go to his flat alone and make love."

"And so you went," said Chess. "Proceed."

Marya threw herself against my pillows and the twelve yards of her skirt billowed and fell back against her. She looked so lovely that I wished I could paint, wished I could put the picture on canvas and keep it.

"Men like Laurence," she said, "never understand when a girl really means what she says. For so long, Laurence has heard girls say No when they mean Yes, and so he has become a little stupid; for him it has become impossible to judge when a girl really is not going to give him what he asks. I told him until I was tired of telling him, and still he did not believe—and so I thought that I must prove it."

"And so?" asked Chess.

"And so I went to his flat. He had challenged me: he said that I was afraid of him. Afraid? I, who know well how to manage passionate men of my own country—afraid? I tried to make him understand that I was not in the least afraid, but he would not believe me—and that made me angry."

"And so?" said Chess again.

"And so I went to his flat. Tonight; alone with him. We went there, and it was all very old-fashioned, I think; he put on music, he put down the lights, he poured out the drinks. It was easy to see how many times he had done all this before; it was very interesting to see how easy he thought it was. He became amorous. When I thought that he was excited enough, I went with him into the bedroom. I asked for another drink, and when he went to get it, I had only to lock the bedroom door quietly, and walk down the fire escape." She rose and stretched sleepily. "He did not, I think, enjoy being left at such a moment, but it will show him that there are one or two women, at least, who do not wish to take lovers."

She walked into the corridor and we heard her a moment later in the bathroom, cleaning her teeth—an act she invariably performed before beginning to undress. Chess and I looked at one another, found nothing to say, and lay silent as Marya undressed in the next room. Then she came into our bedroom and looked at me.

"I am sorry that you worried for me," she said, "but you should have remembered something: that I am a Catholic and it is a deadly—"

"For Pete's sake," I shouted, "will you dry up and go away and let everybody sleep?"

Marya went.

Chapter Seven

The next morning was chaotic. Our alarms didn't wake us, and when at last we got up and hurried through our dressing, we were held up by the constant ringing of the telephone.

The first caller was Laurence Gale. Marya, receiver in one hand and a cup of coffee in the other, stood listening to what seemed an endless speech, to which she replied at last with a brief statement to the effect that she never wanted to see him again.

The next call was from Stephen to Chess, to tell her that he was not as proud as he had imagined himself to be, and asking if he could take her to my mother's party. Chess said no, but I noticed that she lost the somewhat pugnacious expression she had worn since their quarrel.

Then, just as I was leaving the house, Uncle Philip rang me up.

"Thought I'd missed you," he said. "Your phone was busy."

"I'm sorry; people kept ringing up."

"Got a moment?"

"Not really. I was going to ring you from the office to see if you were back."

"I got back late last night," he said. "Well, I'll be brief. Two things. First, a message from your mother."

"Well?"

"She wants to know if she can hire the two young men who acted as waiters at your party. She needs them tomorrow."

"I'll go and ask them. I'll leave a message at Preston's if they're not there."

"Good. Second: are you free after office?"

"Yes."

"Then I'll call for you. Ever heard of Lanzarote?"

I frowned. I hadn't time for puzzles.

"One of the Canary Islands?" I hazarded.

"Yes. Also the name of this new and controversial Spanish painter."

"Oh—the exhibition at the Academy? "

"Yes. Will you take me and show me the finer points?"

I grinned; this was an old joke.

"I'd love to," I said.

"Fine. I'll be outside the office this evening. 'Bye."

He rang off, and I swallowed a mouthful of coffee on my way through the kitchen; then I grabbed my gloves and my coat and my bag and was off down the stairs and out of the house. I went into Preston's; Basil and Joe were both there and

I hurriedly put before them my mother's request. They both agreed to go, and I left them my mother's telephone number and told them to get in touch with her, and took to my heels and ran for the bus.

When I left the office at five o'clock, Uncle Philip was sitting outside in a taxi, waiting for me. He got out and handed me in and patted my hand and said that he was glad to be looking at me once more.

"I wanted to see you, too," I told him. "I've got something to tell you. Something to ask you."

"Something important?"

I thought of poor little weedy, insignificant Mr. Flower, who had never been important during his lifetime.

"Yes, very important," I said.

"Go ahead; I'm listening."

"Not now. When we're having dinner."

" Oh, we're having dinner?"

"You're taking me to that nice little place in Soho."

"I am?"

"Yes. Did you see my mother last night?"

"No. She telephoned about this and that, and then asked me to ask you about the waiters. Did you fix it?"

"Yes. Look"—I nodded towards the Park— "aren't the trees looking lovely?"

"They are," he agreed, "but I didn't think you'd notice it. At your age, you don't usually see the Spring; you feel it."

"You mean you're too old to feel it?"

"We don't have to go into that," he said. "I simply mean that at my age, one drinks in, greedily and consciously, all the Spring freshness and beauty, all the tender greens, the sheen on the grass. Every Spring, at my age, means one more miracle."

It was my turn for some hand-patting.

"You needn't fret about being old," I told him. "You'll look terribly dis-tan-gy, with a nice, interesting face."

"Thank you."

The taxi drew up outside the Royal Academy and we entered the building to find ourselves behind a long line of girl students; we had unfortunately hit on the same day as—their identical blazers declared—the Grant Adams College. Thirty strong, they seemed to group themselves round every picture that Uncle Philip and I wanted to see.

"We could come some other time," I suggested hopefully.

"After paying to come in?" Uncle Philip sounded outraged. "Did you expect to have the place emptied for us?"

"No, but—"

"Look at that." Head on one side, Uncle Philip drew away from a large picture and inspected it critically. " I like it. Do you?"

I had been studying the catalogue; I looked up at the picture before which he was standing.

"Yes," I said at last. "I ... I more than like it. It's . . . it's wonderful."

"You think so?" His pleasure was so great that one would have thought that he had painted it himself.

"Just shows you, Denny. Without any of Madame Narvik's grounding, I picked out the best picture in the room. What I like about it is the Madonna's face; so many of these painted Madonnas look to me either smug or secretive. But this one . . . this one looks as though she really could have been the Mother of God. She looks . . . what's the word? Rapt."

He was looking rapt himself; so much so, that after a time I left him gazing, and wandered down the room and stopped in front of a far less successful painting. Before Uncle Philip got too enthusiastic about Lanzarote, I thought, letting my eyes rest on a brown lake surrounded by blue trees, he ought to take a look at this.

I turned to beckon to him, but found that he was no longer standing where I had left him. He had moved on, and in his place was a large, broadly-built man in a light grey suit and overcoat, with greyish hair and a deeply tanned face.

He turned away from the picture, and for an instant our glances met—and then he looked away. While I . . .I suppose I turned away, but the next few moments aren't very clear in my mind. When I next thought about pictures, I found that I was still standing in front of the brown lake. The Grant Adams College filed in, and I stepped back to allow them to pass me. Behind them, walking slowly, hat in hand, came the grey-haired man. He passed me, and once more we looked at one another. Then he had walked on. The room, the walls, the pictures seemed to recede. I stood where I was and fought down the flood of conjecture that was filling my mind. It was impossible, I told myself. I was crazy. This was the result, I decided, of trying to put a murder out of one's mind; it went down and then came up again in a series of lurid imaginings.

But ... I had to see him again.

He was standing a little way off, and his back was towards me; his hands were clasped behind him, his hat held loosely between them. I moved slowly from picture to picture, approaching him, appearing to consult my catalogue, but seeing nothing—nothing but a blur of print.

The Grant Adams College reached him; he stepped back, as I had done. They passed, but he did not move forward again; he stood where he was, and I went forward a few steps and stood beside him, staring at a picture and counting the moments, forcing myself to wait until I could turn and face him naturally.

I turned. Our glances met and held—and this time, I looked for . . . what I was looking for. Then I moved on, leaving him where he was.

I stopped before a highly-polished door; in one corner was his reflection, and I watched him and saw that he was standing where I had left him. He was looking at me. Looking, and looking, and looking . ..

I looked round for Uncle Philip. He had walked into the next room, and now he came strolling back, side-stepping as he passed the students. I saw him pass the man in the grey suit, saw him lift a hand in a casual salute, saw the man return it.

My heart began to beat in a heavy, thudding way. Uncle Philip came up to me, and stopped.

"Enjoying it?" he asked.

I was feeling breathless, and speech was difficult.

"Who," I asked, "is that man?"

"Which man?"

"The one you made a sort of salute to just now."

"Oh—him? Business friend of mine," he said. "The trouble with this Lanzarote fellow, Denny, is that he's too uneven. One moment a masterpiece; the next, something you'd see at a kindergarten end-of-term exhibition. Look at this one, for example."

I was not looking. I was not listening. The man had passed behind us. I waited until he had walked a few paces, and then I left Uncle Philip and followed him. He paused in the opening that led to the next gallery, and I came up to him. I did not pause, but as I passed him, I raised my eyes and looked, for a second or two, clear into his.

And then I found the nearest seat and sat on it and began to tremble.

It couldn't be. But it could be. It must be. I couldn't, I couldn't, I couldn't be mistaken. I had seen those eyes before. I had seen that nose before: short, blunt, with rather wide nostrils: a nose not at all like my mother's dainty little tip-tilted one; a nose at which I'd gazed often enough in my mirror, gazed at with pride. An Irish nose. An O'Connell nose. And the O'Connell eyes, which my mother, who called herself O'Connell, had never had; eyes widely spaced, in shape rather narrow, in colour greenish. My eyes. My nose. The O'Connell features. I had them.

He had them.

I rose. My knees felt weak, and I was still trembling, and my heart was beating so fast that the sound seemed to fill my ears. I might be crazy . . . but I had to know. I had to know.

He was standing at the end of the room, and he was looking at me—openly, lingeringly . . . hungrily. I don't know what I looked like, but I saw him move suddenly towards me.

I waited. Not as tall as Uncle Philip, but strong— oh, how broad and how strong. A big man; with his blunt nose and broad face, a big Irishman.

O'Connell was coming . . .

He stopped in front of me, and we looked at one another—I don't know for how long. I would have liked to have said something, but I couldn't; I suppose he couldn't either, so we just looked. Then I heard his voice—very deep and very gentle; a coaxing voice.

"Well, Cathy?"

Cathy. Not Denny. Not Denise. My Irish name: Cathy.

I made a tremendous effort.

"Hello," I said. I was shaking, and then I found my hand

in one of his, and my trembling stopped. Someone came to stand beside us, and I heard Uncle Philip's voice; it sounded a long, long way away.

"I see you two have got acquainted," he said.

O'Connell spoke without taking his eyes off my face.

"She's lovely, lovely," he murmured.

I wasn't, but I knew he thought so.

"Lovely indeed," said Uncle Philip. "I must present you to her. Denny, this is the business friend I was . . ."

He stopped. I suppose he saw that for the moment, it was no use. He patted our shoulders and then he turned and went away and left us alone. Alone with the Grant Adams College—and Lanzarote.

Chapter Eight

"You could have come long ago," I said. "Long, long ago."

My father shook his head.

"No. I had to wait. I had to be sure."

"Sure of what?"

He looked down at his plate. We were dining at his Club—to get a chance to talk quietly, he said. We had certainly got it; in a vast chamber built to accommodate two hundred diners, ours was the only occupied table. The food they were setting before us explained why—but for once, I wasn't interested in what I was eating or drinking.

"Sure of what?" I asked again, and he looked up at me and smiled.

"Sure that I could come back without driving a wedge between you and your mother. I waited twenty-three years. And then . . . your Uncle Philip wrote to tell me that your mother had finally asked you to live with her, and you had finally refused."

"But that was merely putting the situation into words. It

had existed in fact since I was sixteen," I said. "Only when I was sixteen, it wasn't possible to live on my own. Especially," I added, "on that inadequate allowance you made me."

He laughed—his head went back and he shook in his chair.

"You can laugh," I said, "but it was a mingy sum."

"It was meant to be," he said, sobering.

"Why?"

"Because—again—I didn't want to drive a wedge. I wanted to give you something, because I was your father, but I didn't want to give you enough to make you independent of your mother. I had to be careful. I'd put myself in the wrong once; I wasn't going to do it again."

"Did you—"

"Eat your dinner; you've touched nothing."

"I'd rather talk. No,"—I corrected myself—"I'd rather listen to you talking. You've got a lot to tell me."

He gave a slow smile.

"You know pretty well all you need to know."

"I don't know the first thing about anything."

"You know your mother. So much I learned from your Uncle Philip."

"Yes," I agreed, "I know my mother."

"And knowing her, and being—Philip said—like me, I knew you'd grow to understand that all they said about me wasn't true."

I leaned forward, elbows on the table, chin on my hands, intent and absorbed.

"But you *did* leave her," I said.

"I did. And with the baby, just as they said. And with no visible means of support, as the newspapers stated. I upped, and I left her. And you."

"But you didn't quarrel."

"No. So much you know, too. She doesn't quarrel. And one thing I'll say about her before I go any further: she didn't cheat. When I married her, she was just what she was, just what she remained, just what—if my guess is correct—she remains to this day: herself. If I'd used my inward eyes, or the good sound sense God gave me, I would have seen ... I was going to say I would have seen the real woman behind the false one, but—"

"—but you mean the false woman behind the real one. I know. Go on."

"She didn't, as I said just now, cheat. She loved me, and she gave me, for about a year, all that any man in love has a right to ask. She was young and sweet and yielding and lovely and tender."

"And then I was born, and she stopped being a wife, and signed on for the Madonna-with-child part."

He looked at me for a moment, and then he smiled; my tone, calm and factual and free from the smallest trace of bitterness, reassured him.

"You know her well," he commented. "You're harsh, but you're right." He lit a cigarette, and then belatedly remembered to offer me one; I shook my head.

"In spite of her tremendous professional success," he went on, "she's a much better actress off-stage than on.She played perfectly the part of a wife—for a time. She played with equal perfection the part of a mother for a time. And then—"

"I think I know," I said, "but I'm not sure: misunderstood woman, other man?"

"Both those," said my father, "but there was something more. When I married her, she'd only just begun her career as an actress. I knew very little about the profession, but I knew good acting when I saw it, and I knew she wasn't very good. I thought she'd play at it for a time, have children and then decide to leave the stage. But I'd left out a great many important factors. First, even if she wasn't a great actress, she was a very engaging one, and she was distractingly pretty . . . and she screened well. Second: far from becoming less interested in the stage as time went on, she became more so. She could feel, I suppose, or she could see how far she would go—upwards. She could see, long before I could, that she'd made a mistake in tying herself up at eighteen to a hulking great Irishman who'd never hit it off with her theatrical friends."

"And who couldn't help her to get to the top." Once more I spoke without emphasis.

"Yes. Every time she married again," he said slowly, "it was a sort of . . ."

"Consolidation. And so you went away?"

"Yes, I went away. I would have hung on, but there was nothing to hang on to. There's something . . . there's something unnerving about going on living with someone who—"

"I know," I said.

"Yes, I suppose you do. She told me, very softly, very sadly, that it was all over, and by that time, I knew her well enough to understand how and why. I hadn't heard the calculating machine ticking over, but it had been going all the time. She'd worked out that I was no use to her, and that was that. Final. Finished. I could have fought, I suppose, but I didn't want to fight to keep her. Only you."

"Why didn't you take me?"

I saw his face harden.

"That was my biggest mistake," he said. "God knows I wanted you. But she was still playing the perfect mother—and you were only fourteen months old and I believed, God forgive me for my blazing stupidity, that she'd be a better mother than I'd be a father." He gave a slow, grim smile. "To look at me now," he said, "I suppose you'd find it hard to believe that in those days I didn't have much confidence in my own judgment. Perhaps my marriage had something to do with it—or it might have been that my damned Irish sentiment misled me; I wouldn't know. All I know is that I thought it out and decided that it was better to leave you with her, and let her divorce me. I came to the conclusion that the divorce in itself wouldn't harm you, because you were too young to have known me, or known who or what I was. All that could have hurt you was the pull between the two of us: father and mother. So I made up my mind I'd leave the two of you. Perhaps I'd caught a bit of the theatrical atmosphere myself, because I let it look as though I'd walked out on her and left her with no means of support. I knew she'd already chosen the next support."

There was silence, and then he began to speak again.

"As you grew up," he said, "I wondered how much you'd begin to understand. Philip never let me get out of touch, and I gathered from him that you were beginning very early to lay your own bets. It was . . . it was exciting to feel that I'd gambled, but hadn't lost you. Thousands of miles away from me, an O'Connell was growing up to be like her father ..."

"But you could have come sooner," I challenged him once more.

"No. This was the moment. She was free of husbands, she had come to London to be near you, she had taken a flat which she hoped you would share with her—and you would have none of it. So I decided that this was the moment at which I could come back. You were engaged, and I wouldn't have much time with you. So I came."

"And that meeting in the Academy," I said, "was a bit more theatre."

"I couldn't bear to come face to face with you all at once. I couldn't bear to be led up to you: 'Mr. O'Connell, sure and this is your lovely daughter . . .' No. I wanted to take it slowly. And when I saw you there, and saw that you had seen me and that you were coming slowly to realise who I was . . . Catherine, that was a great moment for me."

We sat looking at one another, grinning. I don't know what the waiters thought of us. I thought I was going to burst with happiness.

"Can I live with you?" I asked.

"Doesn't that depend," he asked, "on when you're planning to be married? Incidentally," he added casually, "I've met him."

"Met . . . met him?" I repeated blankly.

My father's eyebrows went up.

"He didn't tell you?"

I felt my colour rising.

"He will," I said as calmly as possible. "I haven't had his letter yet."

"Then he ought to start using these new-fangled air mails," commented my father dryly. " It's more than two weeks since we met. I did feel at the time, mark you, that I wasn't making a very favourable impression on him. And he," he went on blandly, " didn't make a very favourable impression on me. Where did you pick him up?"

"He's all right," I said.

"No, he's not," said my father. "What's more, you know it. What's more, you don't like my saying so." He drew a deep, satisfied breath. "Now I feel like a father."

"Now you sound like a father."

"And fathers have to keep their noses out of their daughters' business? Well, yes; ordinary fathers who've had fifteen to twenty years cracking the whip. I've missed all that fun—and when I say missed it, I mean missed it. Your Uncle Philip deputised for me."

"I love him dearly," I said.

"I know you do. Now say those four words again, with as much fervour, but this time with reference to that chap out in Singapore."

I looked at him.

"I did love him—I think," I said at last. "Or perhaps I was a bit lonely at the time. I think we were both lonely, in fact."

"And now?"

"It would be all right," I said, "if we could write better letters. But after the first few weeks, when he'd finished telling me about his first impression of the country, and when I'd lost touch with his sister after her marriage, the ..."

"Then it began to peter out?"

"In a way."

"If I offered you a trip out there to see him, what would you say?"

There was a long silence.

"I . . . wouldn't go," I said at last.

"I see." My father waited until I had poured out his coffee and handed it to him. "Well, let's leave it to simmer for a bit. You're here and he's there and so there's no danger of your rushing into anything. Now tell me about these girls you live with."

"Later. Why didn't you ever come to Madame Narvik's?" I asked him.

"Madame . . . ? Oh, that place in Florence? I've told you: I wanted to wait for the right moment, and the right moment wasn't just then. The right moment is now, when I can't be accused of having made trouble between you and your mother."

"Are you going to see her?"

He ground out his cigarette slowly.

"Yes," he said. "Your uncle's going to arrange it."

"When?"

"She's giving this house-warming party tomorrow. I shall be there, and Philip and I are going to take her out to dinner afterwards."

"Without me?"

He looked up and smiled gently.

"I think so. I thought ... I preferred it that way."

" Because you didn't want it to look like a family reunion?"

He looked at me for a little while, studying me. I waited until he spoke.

"It isn't," he said at last, "a family reunion."

"I know. But does she know?"

"Isn't she on the point of remarrying?"

"The papers say so. I was going to ask Uncle Philip, but he went to Brussels."

"Perhaps she waited to see whether you would live with her, and—"

"But now you're back, won't she play the role of wronged-but-forgiving woman? That means our being together, the three of us. You'd be the repentant husband, I'd be the happy daughter with two parents at last, and she'd be the woman who took you back for my sake."

"You sound . . . frightened," he said.

"Not for myself. For you."

"Cathy, look at me," he said.

I looked at him. About fifty, broad and strong and in complete command of himself. A man no woman could fool.

"I came back," he said gently, "to you; not to your mother."

To my horror, I found tears welling up and threatening to overflow. In panic, I fought them down.

"Perhaps I'm jealous," I said at last.

"Perhaps you are," he said. "If you are, I'm glad. I'd like you to be jealous—a little. Have you," he asked, "ever loved her?"

I took my time.

"I don't know," I said at last. "Like you, I've understood her, I think. Once I used to be proud of her . . . not proud of her, exactly, but of who she was. After I'd grown up, she didn't ever try to make me do anything I didn't want to do. She tried, but if she saw she wasn't going to succeed, she didn't go on. She'd always rather give up something than admit she hadn't brought it off. And that made things easy, I think, for both of us. But love . . . ? She isn't really an easy person to love. For men, yes, for women . . . no. I had a feeling, always, that if I ever reached out to her for anything—anything important, she . . . she wouldn't have it to give. It wouldn't be there. If you don't think it's a silly way of putting it, I always felt that if I asked for bread, I'd get . . . not a stone, but a piece of cake."

"No," said my father after a time. "I don't think that's a silly way of putting it."

Later, he put me into a taxi and sent me home. He wanted to see me to the flat, but we decided that this way looked more natural, more father-and-daughter. He said that he would call for me the next day to take me to my mother's party; then he gave the taxi driver some money and I was driven away.

As I put my latchkey into the door of the house, I glanced purely from habit at the ground floor windows. In one was a light.

And I remembered for the first time for many hours that there had been a murder here, and that Mr. Flower was dead.

Chapter Nine

I don't suppose I shall ever forget my mother's house-warming party. Looking back, I can see that on that evening a number of things were decided, and a number of things begun.

But when I went into the glittering drawing room on my father's arm, I wasn't thinking in abstract terms; I was trying to prevent everybody present from knowing that I was on the point of bursting with pride.

If I'd been asked to state the qualities I wanted in a father, I would have mentioned, without hesitation, several things I felt to be essential—but the first essential would have been humour. Not the obvious kind; I didn't want that. Not the joking kind. Just the quiet kind that showed in a momentary gleam in the eyc; that could be read by an instant's exchange of glances. Humour: the quality my mother had never in the slightest degree possessed. She laughed in her soft, pretty way at people's jokes, and she often spoke warmly of the need to keep always, but always, a sense of humour as part of the armoury of life—but she was incapable of finding the grain of fun that could sometimes lie buried at the bottom of some unfunny situations.

Humour. In my father, I had found what even Uncle Philip, perfect in all other ways, had lacked: the grave, attentive face, the sober, respectful listener's pose which led you to believe that what you were saying was the quintessence of wisdom . . . until you saw, behind the serious glance, the wicked gleam that brought you up on the instant and revealed to you, without the need for a single word, the holes in your logic.

Humour, to round out a perfect father. On his arm I entered my mother's drawing room, so happy, so proud that the room seemed to swim before my eyes.

Then I withdrew my hand from my father's arm and let him go forward to meet my mother.

He had to go a long way. One of the things I liked about my mother's parties—and she was famed for their perfection—was their restfulness. In whatever house she entertained, she judged exactly how many people would make a good party, and how many would constitute a crush. In an age in which most hostesses gave cocktail parties, filling a room to capacity and then letting the guests shriek it out, my mother gave receptions. There was ample space for guests to move about; there were chairs to sit on, and everyone could converse in normal tones. At one end of the room, my mother held court. She never circulated; guests had to make their way across to where she was sitting, and she greeted them and sent them on their way to enjoy themselves—and enjoy themselves they did. The drinks were superlative, and for those who cared to eat, there were countless little sandwiches with a variety of fillings. Guests formed small groups or got into a corner with friends for a confidential chat, and the atmosphere was one of informal enjoyment.

Standing in the middle of the room, I picked out people I knew. Stephen was in one corner, Edward in another; the two were glowering at one another, and Chess was pretending she wasn't enjoying every moment. Her father had buttonholed a Cabinet Minister and her mother was presiding over a small party of foreigners visiting England to study current trends in drama. Marya was the centre of a talkative group near the door; a short distance away stood Laurie Gale, gazing at her over intervening heads and trying in vain to get her attention. Mr. Annuzio was edging towards an up-and-coming screen star named Elspeth Bruce.

I watched my father as he went easily, slowly, almost casually across the room. A slight hush fell, and then talk broke out again, but a great many heads remained turned to watch his meeting with my mother.

She looked so lovely that—as always—I felt torn between a helpless sense of waste and a realisation that nobody can have everything. She had most things; perhaps she didn't need a heart as well.

He was almost up to her, his face grave, polite, but with a faint smile beginning to touch his lips. I heard a voice behind me, but I was too absorbed to turn.

"This," said Portholes softly over my shoulder, "must be making you very happy."

"Hush," I said.

He had reached her. She greeted him as she had greeted all the others—still seated, one small white hand outstretched. To my surprise and delight, my father took it, bent over it and put it briefly to his lips.

"Done like a true Spaniard," commented Portholes. "A graceful race, the Irish. It's a pity about their other qualities."

That brought me round to face him.

"Such as?" I asked.

"Their stability," he said smoothly, "and their cool common sense, their . . . Ah, allow me."

He took two glasses of champagne from a tray and I saw that the waiter holding it was Joe. I smiled at him, and he gave me his usual wide, cheerful grin.

"Nice little place your mother's got here," he said. "That your father, Miss?"

"Yes. He's just back from the East."

Joe glanced at my mother and then gave me a brief wink.

"Bet he stays around," he said as he left us.

I turned back to Portholes, to find him looking in surprise from Laurie Gale to Marya.

"They've quarrelled?" he asked.

"Yes."

"When and how?"

I opened my mouth to give him an expurgated version—and then closed it again. For I had remembered that Marya, in selecting Laurie Gale, had cut herself off temporarily from her other escorts. There were without doubt many in the group surrounding her who had realised that the field was open once more . . . and Portholes would no doubt realise it too. But the situation had changed a little, I reminded myself, since Portholes had first presented himself at our door.

The situation had changed—and so, I understood with a sinking heart, had I. Portholes was no longer an incubus getting in my way night after night at the flat. He had become, I saw clearly for the first time, a friend. I had done more than grow accustomed to him; I had grown to ... to like him.

And now Marya was free, and I had no means of guessing what Portholes was going to do about it.

Beyond strolling to the edge of her group and sending her a few casual remarks, he did very little. His chief interest seemed to lie in my mother, and he walked beside me as, my father having drawn a little away, I went over to speak to her.

"Denise darling." She inclined a cheek; I bent and kissed it and she patted the empty space beside her on the sofa. "You look pale; did your father keep you up late last night?"

"Not very late," I said.

"Uncle Philip wanted you to be surprised; he met your father in Brussels, and they arranged it all. Kevin ' ' —she addressed my father and he came up to us— " this child looks so much like you, don't you think? "

My father studied me critically. "Here and there," he said.

" Ah—Philip."

Uncle Philip, coming up, apologised for his lateness and then pulled my hair.

"How?" he asked.

"She's very well," my father said.

I was watching a man who had just come into the room: the man rumour and the press said my mother was to marry. He sent a glance across the room; it rested for a moment on my father, and something in the look told me, and probably told my father too, that he knew who he was.

I rose from the sofa and took one of the sandwiches Portholes had brought; biting into it, I saw my mother's hand go out to greet the newcomer. I saw the upward glance she gave him—cool and sweet; nothing whatsoever in it, one would have said, of reserve. But I knew her, and I knew that the man bending over her hand had sensed a change. He took a drink from Joe's tray and moved a few paces away to ponder; pondering, I could have told him, wouldn't help him now. He was out, and it was my turn to ponder.

"You're very dreamy this evening," remarked Portholes after a time.

"I'm sorry. Did you say something?"

"Several times. Have you noticed—"

He stopped. My mother had been speaking to Elspeth Bruce; we hadn't heard what they were saying until my mother's voice lifted on a note of astonishment.

"Murder?" she said. "Nonsense, Elspeth."

Elspeth turned to stare at me.

"But surely—" she began, in bewilderment.

She paused. My mother had called me.

"Denise, will you come here a moment?"

With the utmost reluctance, I obeyed, and she spoke in a tone half hurt, half incredulous.

"Why didn't you say anything to me about a murder at your house?"

"Murder?" repeated Uncle Philip.

My father had swung round to stare at me.

"Murder?" he repeated.

Their eyes were on me, at first blank and then puzzled and at last, I saw with dismay, angry.

"I can't understand why you said nothing," my mother went on.

"We ... I didn't want to worry you," I said, and knew that the words sounded lame. "We thought it wasn't ... we felt it was nothing to do with—"

"But wasn't the man your landlord?" asked my mother.

"Yes, but—"

"It happened while the three girls were away," Portholes intervened. "They weren't in London until two days after it had taken place."

"It happened on Friday, didn't it? They were in London

on Friday," said my mother.

"Why on earth," Uncle Philip asked me slowly, "did you keep a thing like that to yourselves?"

"You were away," I said. "I was going to tell you when you came back."

My mother spoke again.

"But, my dear Denise, you must have been . . . What time was the murder; do they know?"

"The ... the police think it was about half past three," I said. "We—"

"But you rang me up from the flat at three o'clock!" my mother said. "I remember most—"

The crash of shattered glass brought her to a halt. We turned to see Fergus Maitland going down on his knees to pick up the pieces, muttering apologies as he did so.

"Terribly sorry . . . never was safe in a drawing room." He grinned at Joe, who had bent to assist him. "My fault entirely, Joe; didn't get a good grasp on the glass when you handed it to me."

"That's all right, sir." Joe spoke indulgently. "You just leave it to me."

"This any use?" Portholes proffered his handkerchief and Joe shook his head.

"I'll fetch a cloth, sir; don't you worry about it."

"Thanks." Portholes rose to his feet. "Damned awkward of me, Joe; I'm sorry."

He turned to my mother, and she received his apologies gracefully, but she was not to be diverted from the subject of the murder. The word spread; the murder, indeed, was out. Chess's parents, Marya's father had soon joined us; Chess and Marya and I, lined up like defaulters, had to face a barrage of questions. The other guests gathered round; some had read of the crime, most had not, but of those who had heard of it, not one had imagined it to have any connection with any of us.

It was my father who brought the discussion to a close, but the buzz of excitement remained, and Chess and Marya and I were only too well aware that we had not heard the last of the matter.

"Good-bye, flat," Chess muttered to me under her breath. "What did I tell you?"

"That it would be Good-bye, flat," said Marya gloomily.

"It was nice of Portholes," said Chess, "to drop his glass—but he did it too late. Why couldn't that woman have kept her mouth shut?"

She looked across the room, but her glance was not on Elspeth Bruce; she was looking at Stephen.

"Made it up?" I asked.

"In a way," Chess said. "I told him I'd dine with him to-night."

There was a pause, and I held my breath; this was a good moment for Fergus to ask Marya about her plans for the evening. But he was looking at me.

"No doubt you're having a reunion dinner with your parents, plural?" he said.

"No."

"Then please come out and dine with me," he begged. " I'm anxious to make up for having ruined your mother's polished parquet. Marya, tell her it would be a shame to waste that pretty frock."

"You are lucky to be going with a man," Marya told me. "Me, I have to go with my father. Denny, I think that this murder is going to spoil everything for us."

"Nonsense," said Portholes.

His tone was light, and remained light until we were facing one another across a dining table in a remarkably poorly-lit restaurant. Then he dealt summarily with the matter of ordering, and waved away the waiter.

"And now," he said, putting his elbows on the table and staring across at me with a frown, "explain."

"Explain what?"

"You know quite well what. A murder's committed, and you all refuse to tell your parents. Well, that's not my business. But now I learn that you were in the flat that afternoon. Why in the name of the devil did you keep so quiet about it?"

"I told Chess and Marya."

"And then?"

"They didn't think I'd be doing any good by going to the police."

"You mean that they didn't want you to get mixed up in it, because they knew their parents would make a row about it."

"That, and other things. There wasn't much I could tell them. I mean ..."

He looked at me, his eyes narrowed. He looked completely unlike the relaxed being who had spent so many evenings on our sofa.

"You know something, don't you?" he said slowly.

"No, I don't. I don't know anything. I just heard something, that's all. If I'd thought that telling the police would have helped poor Mr. Flower, I would have—"

"What did you hear?"

I told him. He heard me to the end without once interrupting. When I had finished speaking, he looked at me for some time with a frown, and then he reached into a pocket, took out a pen and a diary and prepared to take down notes.

"Now; again," he said. "Item by item. You got home at what time?"

"About half past one. I bought my lunch on the way."

"Bought it where?"

"In a shop near the office. Then I washed my hair and set it and then telephoned to my mother—"

"—at three o'clock. And it was after that that you heard Mr. Flower come up?"

"Yes."

"Didn't you . . . don't you remember looking at a clock at

all?"

"Not until I woke up after the doze I fell into."

He said nothing for a time. Then:

"But you must have been seen going into the flat? You must have been seen coming out? Didn't you see anybody about? "

"The street wasn't entirely empty, if that's what you mean. There were the usual passers-by, I suppose. All I know is that I got off the bus and walked to the flat and let myself in—and then let myself out again."

"Leaving Flower, poor devil, dead in the kitchen."

I saw the waiter put some food before me, but I didn't feel like eating. Mr. Flower was back again; meek little Mr. Flower who had never, I was certain, hurt anybody; Mr. Flower, who had felt a knife in his back . . .Was there time to feel?

"Couldn't you have spoken about this to your uncle" Fergus was asking.

"He was away. I was going to tell him the whole story when he came back; it was the only thing that made me feel a bit happier. I wasn't going to keep it to myself; I was going to tell Uncle Philip, and ask for his advice. But he came back—"

"—and brought your father with him. And Mr. Flower, and the murder, went by the board," said Fergus. "Yes, I see that." He put away pen and book, picked up his fork and looked at me. "Eat," he said.

"I'm not really hungry."

"Well, try to eat something. And while you're eating, try to remember exactly what Flower said when he talked to this Alice out of the window."

"I've told you: he said there was nobody in the house and—"

"You're absolutely certain about that?"

"Absolutely. Then he said: 'All right; I'll be down.' No. ' O.K. I'll be down.' He explained that he was fixing a washer."

"But you'd be prepared to swear that he said the house was empty?"

"Yes. Will. . . will I have to swear ?" My heart sank. "Will the police ... I suppose I should have gone to them in the first place."

"Yes, you should."

"But what was the use of going to them and telling them—"

"—that the last person, in all probability, who saw Flower alive was named Alice?"

"How could that have helped them?"

"They keep records; they hear your story and perhaps they turn up in their records, in the district, somebody named Alice. Is that a lead, or isn't it? Whether it is or not, they should have been told. Whether the information was going to be of use to them or not . . . they still should have been told. Every smallest scrap of information might have been, and probably is, vital."

"How do I explain why I didn't tell them before?" I asked, and saw a smile on Fergus's face.

"That," he said, " is your worry. And now tell me about Marya and her quarrel with Gale."

"Marya'll tell you. You can take her out to dinner and get the story out of her."

He shook his head.

"I don't know about that. I mustn't act too hastily."

"*Hastily?* How long," I asked, "is it since you moved into our flat and camped in the drawing room in the hope of catching Marya with a free evening?"

"I couldn't give it to you in weeks and days," he said, "but it's a long, long time. And now, you would say, she's free. But now comes the cunning part: do I rush at her crying ' At last, at last! ' Do I?"

"You tell me."

"I do not rush. She will be expecting it, of course. When I don't rush, she will—"

"—rush off with somebody else."

"Quite so." He beckoned a waiter for the bill, and finished his coffee. "Feel like dancing?" he asked.

"No, thank you. Why don't you haul me to the police station and stand over me while I make my statement?"

"That," he said, "is your Papa's privilege. Are you," he asked, as he settled me into the car, "entirely satisfied with your Papa as a Papa?"

I said that I was. I snuggled down into the deep cushions.

"Where are we going?" I asked.

"The Park. There's a very nice view of the moon through the trees."

There was.

"I almost," said Portholes dreamily as we gazed at it, "took you to the Rivoli tonight. Remember the Rivoli?"

I remembered.

"That was where I first saw you," he went on in the same slow, almost absent tone. "When you came in, I thought to myself, ' Well, now . . .' I thought you were with your father; then I heard you call him uncle. I thought of dropping my napkin at your feet, but it didn't seem a very hopeful beginning. I mean, it didn't give any promise of leading anywhere. Then you uttered one word, and I began to see my way. You said Marya. I listened shamelessly, and then I heard you say Chess. So I put two and two together and decided that it must come to three: Marya, whom I'd met at a party by the river, and the two girls she'd told me she shared a flat with."

"Go on," I murmured, still looking at the moon.

"The trouble was: where was this flat? Your uncle was obviously going to take or send you back to it. But where was it?"

"And so?"

"And so I paid my bill and did some telephoning. Where did Marya live? It didn't take long to find out; one call to Chiswick produced the answer."

"And—?"

"And the next thing was to find an excuse. Ring the doorbell and say: 'I am the man who sat at the next table… ? ' Hardly. And then out of desperation was born inspiration. Marya. Who could doubt that having met her, I must love her? Wooing Marya, I could get in; making passes at Denny, I'd get thrown out. Marya was the answer—and all I needed was flowers. I bought from a waiter, at a large fee, two vasesfuls of their expensive table decoration. Then on, Maitland, on to Stacey Square; on to . . ." He peered at me. "Are you asleep?"

"No."

"You're interested, aren't you?" he asked anxiously.

"Yes."

There was a long silence.

"This chap in Singapore—" began Fergus.

"Tomorrow," I said.

"Just as you say."

But tomorrow, I remembered, watching the moon vanish behind a cloud, tomorrow there would also be Alice.

Chapter Ten

I don't know what value my employers put on my services in the normal way, but on the morning after my mother's party and my dinner with Fergus Maitland, my work must have touched efficiency bottom.

I arrived at the office very late, having stepped in a happy daze on to the first bus that pulled up at the bus stop. I asked for a sixpenny fare as usual, and sat gazing at the streets through which we passed, and was not at all perturbed to find them unfamiliar. When we reached the bus terminus, the conductor tapped me gently on the shoulder and broke the news.

"We don't go no further, Miss."

I came back from the clouds and looked up at him. "Mm?"

"End of the road, Miss. 'S far's we go, I'm sorry to 'ave ter tell yer."

" The . . . Oh, good *heavens*! " I was on my feet, stumbling distractedly to the door. " How in the . . ." The conductor put a hand on my elbow and helped me out of the bus.

"Didn't like to disturb you before, Miss; tried once or twice, when you'd overrun your tanner, but I could see you wasn't with us, so to speak."

"But . . . but where *am* I? "

"Take it easy, Miss," he enjoined consolingly. "You'll be a bit late at the office, I dare say, but what's it matter? This is Spring, and I'll bet you we weren't meant to spend it in offices—nor in buses neither, come to that."

"But how can I—"

"Get back where you want to be? Where d'you want to get to, Miss?"

I told him.

"Then 'op on that bus over there—quick. Change at Charing Cross. Off yer go, Miss; quick. An' thanks for the memory," he called after me, as I sped across the street.

I was coldly received at the office. The shock of the reception kept my work up to a reasonable standard until the middle of the morning, when my own affairs once more intruded, and I was wafted in spirit far from commercial matters. My employers, torn between loathing and anxiety, leaned finally to the latter and at lunch time told me to go home and forward them a certificate from the doctor or the psychologist, whichever.

I stood on the pavement outside the office and felt a wave of happiness sweep over me. I was free. Free for the whole afternoon. Free, also, for lunch.

I glanced at my watch: twelve-thirty. There was time to summon somebody to take me out. I could ring my father, or

Uncle Philip ... or Fergus. Uncle Philip, I decided at first, to show him that in spite of having a father, I still loved him. My father, I thought next, because it was exciting to have a father one could call up and coax for a meal. Fergus, I decided at last, because I wanted to hear his voice.

I heard it. It sounded surprised.

"And they didn't sack you?" he asked.

"No. Where shall we meet?"

"What were you thinking of on that bus?"

"This and that. How about that place behind the Strand?"

"What made you—?"

"Hurry," I said, and rang off.

We didn't say much at lunch, but it was nice to be together. When we rose to leave, Fergus came out of a thoughtful silence and frowned down at me.

"Somehow," he said, "I don't like to think of you alone in the flat all the afternoon."

"Why not?" We threaded our way out of the crowded restaurant and I repeated the question on the pavement outside. "Why not?"

"Because—"

"—of what happened to Mr. Flower? What has that got to do—"

" Listen," he broke in, and at the serious note in his voice, I stared at him in surprise.

"You're not really worried, are you? " I asked.

"Yes, I'm really worried."

Something of the Spring seemed to fade.

"Then you won't have to worry for long," I said. "Our parents are all going to get us out of there before the week s out, lease or no lease. Marya's father was on the phone this morning, and this time, she had to listen. The only thing she and Chess and I have to decide is whether we're going to split up, or stick together and find another flat."

"You've got to get out of this one-and soon," said Fergus.

"Don't worry," I said gently. "Nobody's after any of us."

"Please God," said Fergus, and I knew it was a prayer. "Listen to me," he went on. "And listen carefully."

"Well?"

Go back to the flat. Don't answer the telephone. And—"

"—and lock all the doors?"

There was a pause.

"No," said Fergus slowly at last. "Don't lock the doors."

He bent and kissed me. Considering the time and the place, it was a lingering kiss.

"I'll see you this afternoon," he said.

"You mean this evening."

"I mean this afternoon—at the flat."

You mean you're going to give yourself some time off?"

"I mean just that," he said.

Completely happy, I left him and made my way to Stacey Square. When I got to the house, I saw that the builders, so long awaited by Mr. Flower, had at last come—and gone. There was a scaffolding round our balcony and the balcony railing and half the balcony itself had been removed, but there was no sign of any workmen; they were no doubt coming back in the morning to proceed with the job.

Letting myself into the house and going upstairs, I found myself regretting more than ever the prospect of leaving. I had grown—in spite of its grim associations—to like the house. We had all grown to like it. It was home, and we wanted to stay here; with the balcony soon in use, we could have spent some pleasant summer evenings sitting out on it. We wanted to stay—but I knew that we would all be made to leave. Alice had put a powerful weapon into the hands of our parents.

I remembered that Fergus was coming this afternoon, and wondered whether I could bake some scones for his tea. Anybody, I told myself, could mix a ready- mix and put it into the oven.

Anybody, I remembered, who kept ready-mixes handy. We didn't. Never had the meagreness of our larder been so apparent. But there was, I saw, a small packet of self-raising flour. I examined it and found that Chess, following the cookery book's instructions to dip into flour, had taken the words literally— but a foreign flavour, I felt, might improve the scones.

It didn't. Hope went into the oven and despair came out. I could have laid the scones on any shingle beach, and nobody would have noticed the difference.

I put the evidence in the garbage bucket and went into the drawing room and put two teacups on a tray, brooding as I did so. Every girl, I mused, should be first and foremost a cook; cooking was, of all arts, the most essential. At twenty-five, or nearly, to be unable to whip up half a dozen scones ... it was terrible. What man would appreciate a lecture on Goya or Velasquez while he was chipping pieces of his teeth on the lecturer's pastry? What man . . .

But the tea-table looked very nice. It was too early to put on the kettle; it was only half past three.

Half past three . . .

In spite of myself, I found my carefree mood clouding. Depression settled on me; depression, but no sense of fear. Mr. Flower had been murdered, and by the merest chance, I had been close to the tragedy— but it had, I felt, no possible connection with me. I felt pity and horror—but I was not afraid.

But for the first time, I faced the realisation that a murder could not take place so close to us without making ripples that widened and widened until even those not directly connected with the tragedy felt its effects. Mr. Flower had been very little to us—but he had lain dead two floors below us and the police had tramped in and out, and the heads of passers-by still turned to look at the scene of the crime. Mrs. Flower had returned; we had seen the light in her window,but we had not yet seen her—but soon we would have to meet, and every meeting would remind us . . .

I shook myself free of the gloom that was filling my mind, and almost succeeded—but I was aware that in the last few moments I had come to the conclusion that it would be better for the three of us to look for another place in which to live . . . if we were still going to live together. But I didn't think we were. Looking at the facts squarely at last, I saw that several things were going to unite to separate us. Chess had said nothing about Stephen, but I knew that he was once more in the picture; if they came together again, he was not the man to stand around waiting for her to have another fling; he would marry her, and soon. Marya would probably move into her father's house.

For myself ... I didn't know.

I walked to the window and pushed it up as far as it would go; then I dragged a big chair up to the patch of sunlight on the carpet, and sat down and stared out over the ruined balcony, and fell into a dream. I couldn't have mapped out the future, but . . . perhaps others would map it out for me. It was wonderful to sit there, just dreaming . . . dreaming . . .

And so it was that, being deep in dreams, I heard nothing. Nothing but a click—the click of the drawing room door closing. Without fear, I turned; Fergus, I said to myself, had arrived. And as I turned, my only thought was dismay at not having put the kettle on to simmer, so that it would have been ready for me to make the tea.

But what I saw was the back of a man. His left hand was on the lock of the door. In his right hand was a knife.

Chapter Eleven

I know quite well what happens at this point in a great many plays or films in which there has been an element of mystery. I know, and everyone else knows that the villain, having cornered his victim, pauses before delivering the final, the fatal stroke in order to recite a full history of the motive and the method of his previous crimes. As his recital ends, as he approaches his cowering quarry, the curtains of the room part to reveal several police officials with tape- recorders, and the villain is disarmed, handcuffed and taken away. The end.

Nothing of that kind was to happen now. The door was locked. I was alone. Alone with a man who was coming towards me and coming swiftly. Coming to kill.

I made only one sound: one gasping, choked, astounded utterance: his name. I had no coherent thoughts; I had no time for thought of any kind. One look into a pair of eyes—eyes that I had seen only gleaming with laughter, eyes that were now terrifyingly blank and empty—told me that I was facing death. Through my blind panic, struck, for an instant, profound astonishment. I, Denise Catherine O'Connell, was to die like this. I. Myself.

They say that the Irish are hard to kill. Perhaps this is so. He must have thought—if he was thinking at all—that this was going to be harder than walking up behind poor little unsuspecting Mr. Flower and striking one fatal blow. I wasn't Mr. Flower. I was young, and fairly strong. I was quick on my feet, and I had the advantage of knowing the room and everything in it. I knew that he would trip over the cord of the telephone behind the sofa. I knew that the big chair didn't have castors and wouldn't roll, but that the sofa had, and did. I knew that the small chair by the fireplace was top-heavy and would go over backwards, and that the door of the big, ugly sideboard always swung open and blocked the way if anybody bumped into it. I knew all this, and I used the knowledge again and again and again—but I knew that after a time, the advantage would lessen. I would tire, I would trip, and a hand would reach out and grip me . . .

It was a battlefield, and we fought. Once he touched me—his fingers touched, but could not close round my arm, for I turned like a wild creature and bit and drew blood. More than once he managed to seize my skirt or my sleeve, and I heard the sound of tearing, and then there would be only the other sounds: the sound of a man breathing in hoarse, heavy gasps, the sound of a girl panting . . .

He began to change his tactics; speed and strength had failed; guile might trap me.

I fought on, but I fought without hope. Screaming—if I had had the breath to scream—would not help me; there was no one to hear. There was no one to help.

I fought on. From somewhere deep within me welled up a mighty determination to die hard. I would lose, and I would die, and that was incredible—but there would be blood on both sides. Both sides.

He heard the blows on the door, I think, before I did, for he glanced round for an instant. Perhaps he made a rough calculation: the door would hold long enough for his purpose, long enough to enable him to make his escape.

And perhaps it would have done, if I had been my mother's daughter; my mother, who fought with delicate weapons and who gave up easily. But I was my father's daughter, and when at last the door broke and fell and my father could see me, bloody and torn but still fighting, perhaps his O'Connell blood saluted mine.

It was into his arms that I ran, and not into Fergus's—and perhaps that made my father glad, too. It was from his arms that I turned and saw a man, still with knife in hand, backing, backing before the advance of Fergus Maitland and my Uncle Philip and two blue-clad policemen.

I am glad that I screamed a warning. I shall always be glad that I tried to stop him.

"Joe!" I didn't recognise my own voice, half-croak, half-shriek. "Joe! Don't . . . don't . . ."

I think he must have known. He went on backing . . . backing. Then he had reached the open window and given a swift, swooping, twisting movement and stepped out on to the balcony.

In the deadly hush that followed, I heard . . . Oh, God . . . the sound of the fall. And I remember wondering, as darkness began to close over me, why the fall came first and the screams came afterwards. Screams . . . high, prolonged screams.

Darkness fell—but not before I knew that they were the screams of a woman.

Chapter Twelve

I was in hospital for ten days; when I came out, it was not to Stacey Square, but to a flat my father had rented in Knightsbridge; a flat large enough to accommodate not only himself and myself, but also Chess. Marya was living a short walk away, in her father's house; she had had no alternative but to join him, but she had done so only after making certain changes, notably in evicting a lady called Rita and replacing two pretty little Breton maids by two extremely plain, middle-aged German ones.

How far my father was responsible for the letter that came shortly afterwards from Singapore, I shall never be able to find out. It was a short letter; it said merely that two people, drawn together by a moment of loneliness, could read into a pleasant companionship more than was in fact there. I was to be happy—and forget, and he was mine ever. For a girl who had been jilted, I stood up remarkably well.

When I marry Fergus Maitland, which will be on the fifteenth of September, I shall find it hard, if ever he gets above himself, to prevent myself from reminding him of the time he arranged for me to be murdered. For arrange it he did.

It was perhaps because—as he said—it had all seemed too easy.

"It looked absolutely straightforward," he told me at the hospital, when I was well enough to hear the facts. "I was certain it couldn't miss, certain that nothing could go wrong. Your father and your uncle held out for a bit, but I convinced them that this was the surest way of finding out . . . what we had to find out. I didn't have to convince them that we had to act at once; so much they understood."

"Did they—"

"Wait." He stopped me gently. "Let me tell it. Questions when I've finished. Ready?"

"Yes." My hands were in his.

"You see," he said quietly, "when that glass dropped in your mother's drawing room, I knew that my hand had never touched it. Joe, handing it to me, had heard what I'd heard: that you had been in the flat on the afternoon of the murder. The glass dropped from his hand—not mine. One quick look, and I saw that he'd gone as grey as a ghost. I told myself that the time for thinking was afterwards; for the moment, I had to convince him, if I could, that I'd thought it was my fault.

"So that was the first puzzle—but it didn't last long, because an hour later, at dinner, you told me that Flower had looked out of the window and said: ' Is that you, Alice? ' To you, Alice meant only a woman's name. To me, it meant—and it would have meant if I'd been there and heard Flower say it—not a Christian name, but a surname."

"A surname?"

"Yes." He smiled at me. "You see, my mother's maiden name was Allis. A-l-l-i-s."

He paused, but I had nothing to say.

"So from there," he went on, "it was easy. First thing next morning, I saw your father and talked to him. Then we talked to your uncle because your uncle, as a long-standing and highly-respected resident of this country might, we thought, know a few top-ranking policemen. He only knew one—but that was enough. We all went, then and there, to see him, and I said my piece. I said that I wanted to find out whether Joe's surname was Allis—but I wanted to find it out in a way that would frighten him. If he was frightened, I thought, he would act in one of two ways: he'd disappear ... or he would decide to find out how much you knew. So he would question you. He'd had time to do some thinking, and he must, I felt certain, have come to the conclusion that you had looked out of the window that afternoon and seen him. You hadn't told your parents, so he had good grounds for supposing you hadn't gone to the police. You hadn't gone . . . but he must have known that it was only a matter of time before you did. If he didn't decide to disappear, he would have to see you—and we wanted to be there when he did.

"And so we made a plan. A simple plan. A plan so simple that ... it simply didn't work."

"Who made the plan?"

"Your father, your uncle, the high-ranking policeman—

and yours truly."

"I see."

"It's too early to see," Portholes said. "I'm just telling you. First of all, your Uncle Philip went to the shop—Preston's. He strolled in and asked if he could have a word with Joe. Joe was produced, and your uncle said that he'd been asked by your mother to thank him for having acted as waiter and to ask him if he'd go along and do the same at a party she was giving next week. Joe said he would. Your uncle thanked him and strolled out of the shop, but on his way out, he stopped and picked up one of those round tins with a cake inside. He handed the tin to Joe, told him that you had the afternoon off and were expecting a visitor at four o'clock, and asked him to deliver the cake and any other little things he thought might come in handy at a young lady's party. He handed over enough money to cover the transaction, and then departed."

"Leaving Joe with the knowledge that I was off work, and in the flat?"

"Yes. I told you it was simple."

"Go on."

"Well, a short time after your uncle left the shop, a police inspector went in and asked if he could speak privately to Mr. Preston. Mr. Preston led him into a room behind the shop and the Inspector flashed his badge. Preston was shaken, but not unduly; he's an honest man and he had nothing to be afraid of—for himself. What, the Inspector asked, was his nephew Joe's surname?"

"Joe Allis ..." I said.

I closed my eyes and tried not to remember. Joe. Smiling, jolly Joe . . .

"Yes, he was Joe Allis," said Fergus. "Could the Inspector have a word with him? No, the Inspector couldn't, said Mr. Preston; his nephew Joe was out delivering groceries."

Fergus paused.

"The Inspector wasn't taking the case very seriously," he went on after a time. "To him, I dare say we all looked like a bunch of amateurs doing a bit of guesswork. He came out and joined us in the King's Road—your father and your uncle and myself—and made his report. And I made my mistake. My big mistake. You see, I ... I believed him. I mean, I believed Preston. I knew that Joe's job took him out a good deal, and I thought that Preston had told the truth. If I'd been thinking coolly, I would have realised that of course Preston, honest or not, would have lied then to give Joe a chance. But I didn't think of that, and so we accepted the Inspector's statement and we all made our way, without too much haste, to take up our vigil in the flat."

"Were you—"

"We were to leave two policemen posted unobtrusively in the Square; your father and your uncle and I, with two more policemen, were to wait downstairs in the Flowers' flat, watching to see if Joe Allis came. He might come with the things your uncle had ordered for your tea party ... or he might come without them. He might go upstairs and come straight down after delivering his parcels ... or he might not. On our way to the flat, we stopped at the coffee bar and picked up Mrs. Flower; we needed her to let us in. We told her very little, and she told us nothing whatsoever —then, or later.

"And so we got to the house, to wait for Allis. And outside the house . . . was Preston's van. The van Joe always drove."

Once more Fergus paused, and I waited.

"Joe had moved fast," he went on presently. "And he had moved in the open. Perhaps he thought he could kill you and get away, or perhaps he planned to tell a story of having brought something for you from the shop and . . . and found you there . . . dead. We shall never know. And I shall never know how we all got up the stairs and how we got into the room. Five of us—but it was your father who got his weight against the panel and split it at last."

That was the end of Fergus's story, and there is little to add to it. I know that there should be a neat, tied- up solution—but there isn't. All there is is conjecture. Conjecture as to why Mrs. Flower rushed screaming out of the house when the body crashed on to the street outside. Conjecture as to why she gathered Joe's body to her and cradled it against her heart and moaned broken phrases of love. Conjecture as to whether Joe Allis loved her, or whether he felt that marrying her would bring him a comfortable home-with-income and, just around the corner, a coffee bar that could be a gold mine. For although we had never thought that Mr. Flower had possessed many of the world's goods, he had more than enough to tempt Joe

Allis. The police thought it probable that Allis decided to murder first and marry afterwards, but they do not think that he made Mrs. Flower party to the scheme; it was enough for him to know that once Mr. Flower was out of the way, the widow would be very easily won.

None of us has been to Stacey Square since then; none of us, I think, will ever want to. Sometimes I remember my first visit to the flat, and Mrs. Flower's sudden decision to let us have it—a decision that was to cost her lover his life . . .

Marya is trying to get Stephen and Chess together. Chess is trying to keep Marya and Laurie Gale apart. The behaviour of Laurie is a mystery to all: he offers to do penance for his past, to make amends in the future, to foreswear wine and women—with the exception of Marya—and to become a Catholic if she will marry him. My father's comment is that the devil a monk was he.

Portholes thinks that my mother will get my father. I think she probably won't; in the meantime, my father is enjoying every minute of the chase. When I see them together, he returns my gaze with a bland look; behind it I can see awareness, wariness—and amusement. Her line seems to be that they should come together before my wedding, to make things look tidier. My father never discusses the matter with me, but once I put a direct question and got an indirect answer.

"You have to remember, Cathy," he said, "that what a man of my age needs most of all is plenty of exercise. Physical and mental. Keeps him on his toes."

Even Portholes couldn't quite work that out—but of one thing I was able to assure him out of my knowledge of my mother, and that is that when she looks at my father, handsome and alert and vigorous and overflowing with devastating Irish charm, she can't for the life of her make out why she ever let him go.

THE END

The Gentlemen Go By

by

Elizabeth Cadell

"Oh—Florence!" Lorna turned and called, and Florence, on her way into the house, paused and glanced over her shoulder.

"Well?"

"You didn't tell me his name," said Lorna.

"Nicholas."

"Yes," said Lorna, "but there must be some more."

"Nicholas Saracen," said Florence, and went into the house.

And Lorna Salvador, on the terrace, stared after her with the blood draining slowly from her face and her eyes wide and filled with something not far from panic.

Nicholas . . . Nicholas Saracen. He was coming here. He was coming . . . soon . . . now. She would be face to face with him; she would see him, hear him, be near enough to touch him. She felt herself trembling at the thought, and made a desperate attempt to regain her self-command. She forced herself to look forward, and saw their meeting as it would be—a young man coming to meet an unknown woman, a young man anxious to talk about himself and his life. Nicholas—in love.

Nicholas, Nicholas, Nicholas—

The moments passed, but Lorna stood still, quieter now, and with a new feeling welling up from the bottom of her heart. Nicholas—she was free to see him. That was all that she need think about at present. A smile curved her lips; it was tremulous at first, but it grew wider; a light of expectancy came into her eyes and the colour came back to her cheeks. She found herself free from apprehension, and lifted up with pure happiness. Nicholas . . .

Joyously, she went inside to prepare for his arrival.

End of preview.

To continue reading, look for the book entitled

"The Gentlemen Go By" by Elizabeth Cadell.

About the Author

Elizabeth Vandyke was born in British India at the beginning of the 20th century. She married a young Scotsman and became Elizabeth Cadell, remaining in India until the illness and death of her much-loved husband found her in England, with a son and a daughter to bring up, at the beginning of World War 2. At the end of the war she published her first book, a light-hearted depiction of the family life she loved. Humour and optimism conquered sorrow and widowhood, and the many books she wrote won her a wide public, besides enabling her to educate her children (her son joined the British Navy and became an Admiral), and allowing her to travel, which she loved. Spain, France and Portugal provide a background to many of her books, although England and India were not forgotten. She finally settled in Portugal, where her married daughter still lives, and died when well into her 80s, much missed by her 7 grandchildren, who had all benefitted from her humour, wisdom and gentle teaching. British India is now only a memory, and the quiet English village life that Elizabeth Cadell wrote about has changed a great deal, but her vivid characters, their love affairs and the tears and laughter they provoke, still attract many readers, young and not-so-young, in this twenty-first century. Reprinting these books will please her fans and it is hoped will win her new ones.

Also by Elizabeth Cadell

My Dear Aunt Flora
Fishy, Said the Admiral
River Lodge
Family Gathering
Iris in Winter
Sun in the Morning
The Greenwood Shady
The Frenchman & the Lady
Men & Angels
Journey's Eve
Spring Green
The Gentlemen Go By
The Cuckoo in Spring
Money to Burn
The Lark Shall Sing
Consider The Lilies
The Blue Sky of Spring
Bridal Array
Shadow on the Water
Sugar Candy Cottage
The Green Empress
Alice Where Art Thou?
The Yellow Brick Road
Six Impossible Things
Honey For Tea
The Language of the Heart
Mixed Marriage
Letter to My Love
Death Among Friends
Be My Guest
Canary Yellow
The Fox From His Lair
The Corner Shop
The Stratton Story
The Golden Collar
The Past Tense of Love
The Friendly Air
Home for the Wedding
The Haymaker
Deck With Flowers
The Fledgling
Game in Diamonds
Parson's House
Round Dozen
Return Match
The Marrying Kind
Any Two Can Play
A Lion in the Way
Remains to be Seen
The Waiting Game
The Empty Nest
Out of the Rain
Death and Miss Dane

Afterword

Note: Elizabeth Cadell is a British author who wrote her books using the traditional British spelling. Therefore because these books are being published worldwide, the heirs have agreed to keep her books exactly as she wrote them and not change the spelling.